Timeless devotion

by

JN Goulet

JNGoulet2022©copywriter

Prologue

It's an early hot sixth of August in Kyoto Japan. The scars of war can be seen on the landscape of burnt homes and crumbled stone and steel buildings. Very few structures in the city have not been touched by the allied bombing.

Homes and temples were not spared the destruction, except for a small wooden house, where Sakusha Chisato and her fellow Geisha and Maikos live and spent there days trying to survive and train in the worst of conditions.

Little to no food to eat, many of the senior geishas had first choice of any available food, with the maikos and other trainees left to starve or fend for them selves.

Many of the geishas in training had no home to return to, due the war or sold off by their family's. Sakusha Chisato was one the one's who's parents were poor before the war, now they could not afford to feed them selves let alone her. They had two choices; leave her to fend for her self on the street or send her to be come a geisha at the age of fourteen.

Training to be geisha is no easy task; the first two years you're basic a slave to the others who are senior. As the war lingered on it made Sakusha's life and the lower ranked women life more harsh.

The lack of patrons meant the lack of money or food for the women, forcing some of the women to resort to prostitution. Namori Gahou the head mother of the house frowned on prostitution but she allowed the mature geisha's to sell them selves to survive. The maiko's and lower women were not allowed to sell them selves for any amount of food or money.

It's been four years since Japan went to war with the United States, Sakusha is now a young woman who has endured the many trails and hardships. As a Maiko, Sakusha is one step from reaching her goal to be a geisha.

Outside, Sakusha and the other women she trained with were outside staring into the horizon, when a flash of light lit up the sky, then a few moments later the ground shook.

"Sakusha, what was that?" Mouso Isaki one of the other trainees asked her. "I do not know. I have never seen a bomb like that before. We should consult Namori about it." Sakusha suggested.

"Okasan!" "What is it?" Namori replied. "We witnessed a great flash in the sky, then the ground shook." Sakusha tells her. "I did feel the ground shake. You said you saw the sky light up, it must being a new weapon the Americans are using. How many flashes did you see?" Namori inquired. "We saw only one." Sakusha tells Namori.

"If it just one bomb I would not worry.
We have had thousands of bombs
dropped on us. One will not affect the
war effort. Namori assures Sakusha
and the other trainees.

August 15th the Emperor speaks to
his people, bringing tears and anger to
many. Namori and the other geishas
wept in sorrow and in disbelief at
Japan's surrender.

Chapter one

Thunder

A room encased in steel, surrounds warriors who await their orders, not for war but to occupy and rebuild a war-torn country.

These war-weary offices will have a new experience. Four years of fighting have hardened them; now, they must show compassion and patience.

A general and his aide walked into the room, calling to attention. Everyone stands.

"At ease, everyone," commands the general. The officers sit to listen to what the general has to say.

The general's aid begins to speak. "You all know what districts you will be in charge of and where you will set up your camp. Before you leave, the general wants to stress a few issues.

Many of you have been fighting the Japanese since the first day of the war. We are here as an occupying force and do not wish to fall into the same category of brutality as the Japanese were treating others.

Helping Japan to recover from the war will take time. Marshal law will be in place until ordered differently. If you need to hire the locals for any construction project; remember, food is more important than money when you are starving.

The restricted areas are Hiroshima, Nagasaki. Medical personnel only are allowed. The radiation from the bombs will kill you if you stay too long in the area. For example, if you want the blood to flow from your eyes and die a horrible death; that is the place to be.

Under no circumstances are you or any of your men are to go to the island of Hokkaido. The Russians are not on the best of terms with us. We don't need an international incident to happen. Enter that island; a court marshal is waiting for you on your return. That is all. Now take your convoys to your districts."

After the General leaves, the officers make preparations to leave.

"Major Star, what was the meeting about?" Sergeant Kazinski asked him. "It was a reminder on how to treat the locals and a warning on visiting Hiroshima, Nagasaki, and Hokkaido. When the men get their quarters set up, make sure everyone knows to avoid those places I mentioned, or they will be court martial." Major Star ordered. "I will, Sir. Where are we going, Sir?" Sergeant Kazinski asked.

"Kyoto is our destination. Outside the town of Kita-Ku. I'm hoping the roads are passable and the bridges are still intact, or we will have to find another route on this map." Major Star tells his sergeant.

The Major and Sergeant Kazinski are in the lead jeep, followed by fifty trucks filled with men, food, and equipment needed to build the army camp.

The ride to Kyoto is a solemn one for the Major. There is no way for him to avoid seeing the war's toll on the civilian population with bodies of women and children lying on the side of the road, burnt homes as far as the eye can see.

Major Star has seen his fair share of death, a veteran of several island campaigns. It still upsets him when he sees the war's toll on the civilians.

"Major, do you mind if I ask you a question? Tell me to shut up if it's none of my business." Sergeant Kazinski says.

"Go ahead and ask." replies the Major. "Why is a Major in command of a division of men? Normally, the job is for a full bird or higher."

"Politics; I had a soldier thrown in prison for murdering his prisoners." "That doesn't explain why a major is commanding a division." Sergeant Kazinski says.

"He happened to be a senator's son. The Senator had the last laugh screwing up my promotion. I'm here because I speak the language, and the Japanese found out about the trail. They suggested it would be good for public relations if I were part of the occupation force. Here I am. Do you have another question?" Major Star asked his sergeant.

"I do, one more. This map has us driving through the center of Kyoto. Is there a reason why we don't take these other routes? The route through Kyoto is the longest one." Sergeant Kazinski inquired.

"There is; it's all about posturing. We are the victors, and the government wants the people of Japan to know it," explains Major Star.

The convoy rolls along, entering Kyoto; Major Star pays attention to the city's people and buildings, neither looking very welcoming.

"Miss Gahou, what is that sound? It sounds like thunder." Sakusha asked. "I do not know. The house is beginning to shake," she replies.

The women of the geisha house step outside to witness the massive convoy of men and equipment driving down their street.

Miss Gahou and the women of her house stood in silence as they watched the spectacle with heavy hearts.

Chapter two

Humility

Occupied with the camp's construction, Major Star has not had time to survey his main objective, to establish martial law, and assess the inner city's infrastructure. That is soon to begin, with the camp's outer perimeter completed.

The atmosphere at the geisha house are becoming desperate; starvation is starting to take it's toll. Facing starvation, Sakusha decides to venture on her own, fully dressed as a geisha without Gahou's permission.

With martial law imposed in Kyoto, the locals were not allowed on the streets after dark.

Sakusha's secret exit from the house was discovered after the sun has set when Gahou began questioning the other women under her care.

"Mouso have you seen Sakusha? I have been searching for her for an hour." Gahou asked.

"I have not Gahou-san. I noticed her clothes are missing from her room." Mouso stated.

"That foolish girl went on her own to find someone to sell herself. I want everyone to remain in the house while I look for that child!" Gahou ordered the women of the house.

"You cannot venture outside. It will be dark soon; the Americans will arrest you if you are out during curfew." Mouso tells the head mother of the house Gahou.

"I will risk it, just to beat some sense into that child." states Gahou.

Sakusha's disobedience and carelessness cost her when she decides to walk through an alley where large damaged buildings are unstable and can come crashing down any time.

Stumbling through ruble, Sakusha is struck by debris falling from a building rendering her unconscious, where she lay covered with dirt and large wooden beam throughout the night.

That evening Gahou was forced to call off her search because of the American military patrolling the streets.

"Did you find Sakusha?" One of the Maiko's asked Gahou. "I did not. I will continue in the morning." Gahou says. "You could ask the Americans to help look for her." Mouso suggested. "I will not have anything to do with the Americans!" Gahou sternly replies.

The only problem Gahou has with searching for Sakusha in the morning is Major Star and Sergeant Kazinski surveying to town at the crack of dawn.

"Major, a lot of these buildings are ready to fall." states Sergeant Kazinski.

We're going to mark those who are going to be torn down." Major Star says.

The morning sun brightens the shadows making clearer to see, where the Major's eye catches a glimpse of a reflection.

"Sergeant, stop the jeep; I want to check something in the alley." The Major sees the white makeup on Sakusha's face glow in the sun light.

What the Major finds is a partially buried woman under bricks and mortar, stepping through the ruble. "What did you find Major?" Sergeant Kazinski asked.

Discovering the woman still breathing, the Major calls for his sergeant.

"Kazinski! get over here! There's a woman buried under this ruble, and she's alive." "You're Sir, she is alive." Sergeant Kazinski says.

"She won't very long if we leave her under this junk. Give me a hand with this beam on top of her.

I want you to pull her away when I lift the beam." Major Star tells his sergeant.

On the count of three, pull her out. One, two, three! Argh!!@" Major star grunted out lifting the heavy piece of lumber.

"She's free Major; you can drop the beam." Star kneels beside Sakusha's body to examine her injuries closer.

"Major, isn't she one of those geisha hookers?" Kazinski asked.

You're half right, Sergeant. She's geisha, not a hooker. Geisha do not sell their bodies; they are more like entertainers for the rich. This one is young to be a geisha. Under her makeup, I bet she's barely eighteen years old."

"What are you going to do with her? I don't think there are any hospitals in the area." says Sergeant Kazinski.

"If there are, most of the doctors are at Hiroshima and Nagasaki. We'll take her back with us; our medic will look at her injuries." says the Major.

The Major is met at the gate by his lieutenant. "Sir, who is she?" "I don't know. I found her beneath some ruble. Is there a problem?" the Major asked his subordinate. "No. I happened to see you entering the gate, so I'd advise you the Japanese liaison has arrived."

"Perfect timing. Have the Liaison meet me at the medical tent." Major Star orders.

chapter three

Humble perspective

"Sir, this is Capitan Hito Soyu." Lieutenant Gloster informs Major Star.

Capitan Soyu salutes, with the Major acknowledging a salute in return.

"Captain Soyu, since you're my liaison, this woman will be your first task. I believe she is a geisha. I found her unconscious in an alley under some rubble." Star explains.

Captain Soyu examines the young woman's pale face and her clothing. "She is not a geisha yet. The red clothing that stands out around her neck says she is a maiko." Captain Soyu explains.

"Do you know where she comes from?" Star asked the captain. "I do not. I am not from Kyoto," replies Captain Soyu. "That's strange. I would have thought command would have sent someone familiar with the area." the Major says to Soyu.

"My people suggested it would be someone with no affiliation with the town, in case someone might seek vengeance against my family for helping.

How bad is this woman injured?" Soyu asked the Major. The medic's first look at her didn't find any broken bones, except for a nasty bump on her head. We'll know more when they remove the makeup and her clothing. I have a nurse coming to remove her heavy dress and makeup, so the doctor can adequately check her."

The next afternoon Sakusha's eyes open to her surprise. She is not in her kimono, but olive drab pants and shirt.

"Where am I?" Sakusha says. Looking beneath the blanket, her eyes open, fearing her violation.

"Help! Help me!" Sakusha cries out. The nurse rushes to her. The nurse struggles to hold Sakusha down; not understanding the Japanese language is a blessing because what was coming from Sakusha's mouth was not lady like for geisha.

"What's going on?" says the Major. "Sir, she will not settle down. Help me hold her down." says the nurse.

Major Star begins to speak to Sakusha in her language. " Relax, you are not in danger. Nothing happened to you; your clothes are on the chair. I found you hurt, so I brought you here. Can you tell me your name?" Major Star asked Sakusha.

" I am Sakusha Chisato. Where am I?" Sakusha asked. "You're at an American army camp. When you're well enough, I'll take you home. Are you hungry?" the Major asked.

A smile for the Major and one blush expression from Sakusha come with the growling of her stomach replying to the Major's question.

"Nurse, can you go to the mess tent and see if the cook has any leftovers? I will keep an eye on Miss Chitosa."

"Captain Soyu, good timing, our guest has awakened. Miss Chitosa, this

Captain Soyu, he will be my liaison between you and your fellow Japanese people." Major Star informs Sakusha.

The nurse returns with a cabbage and beef soup with bread for Sakusha. The smell of the broth overwhelms her senses to a point where she begins to cry.

"Nurse, what's the overall condition of Miss Chitosa's health?" asked the Major. "Except for the bump and bruises, she's slightly emaciated from starvation." the nurse tells the Major.

"Sergeant Kazinski!" Star calls out. "You called Major." "Yes." Major Star hands his Sergeant a slip of paper. "I want you to load these items in my jeep." "As you say Major," replies Kazinski.

"Miss Chitosa, when you're ready, I will drive you home. You don't have to rush eating. If you want more food, I'm sure I can find more." Major Star says.

Sakusha nods; she would like seconds holding out her bowl.

With her stomach filled, Sakusha, Captain Soyu, Major Star with Sergeant Kazinski as the driver hop in the Majors jeep to return Sakusha home.

Arriving at the home for the geisha's, Sakusha finds a spastic head mother and geisha Namori Gahou.

"Chisato, where have you been? I searched for you for two days!" Gahou's concern turns to anger when she sees the Major.

Commanding Sakusha to get in the house, Gahou begins shouting at the Major.

"Captain Soyu, my Japanese is a little rough; she is speaking too fast for me to understand." says the Major. " It's not good. She's accusing you of taking advantage of the maiko." Captain Soyu explains. "Can tell her I did not do anything to her?" the Major says. "it will not help. The woman is hysterical with a distaste of Americans."

Finishing with her ranting, Gahou storms back into her house.

"Major, what do you want to do with these sacks in the jeep?" Sergeant Kazinski asked. "Leave them by their door." Major Star tells his Sergeant.

Gahou's ranting does not end with the Major; Sakusha is getting an earful for leaving the house, frightening the life out of her with worry.

Once everything settled in the geisha's household, Gahou sees Sakusha dragging a large bag of rice to the kitchen.

"Chisato, where did you get that?" Gahou asked her. "The Americans left it at our door. There is a bag of flour I still have to drag to the kitchen. "Sakusha tells Gahou.

"Why did you not tell me the American left the food at our door?" Gahou asked. "You never gave me a chance!; Between you insulting the American and scolding me, I never had a chance.

Another thing, the American's did nothing but save my life. The Major found me injured under a fallen building.

Knowing you, he was on the receiving end of your choice of words and insults. The Major does speak our language, so I am sure he understood you well." Sakusha informs Gahou.

A wave of humility envelopes Gahou's soul, disgracing herself by insulting the person who saved one of her trainees and giving food to help her house has left her drained.

chapter four

The Start

"Gahou, where are you going?"
Sakusha asked. "I want you and the
others to remain in the house while I
am gone," Gahou replied. "O.K. You still
have said where you are going," says
Sakusha.

"I am going to the American's camp. I
need to apologize for my many insults."
"You know the American's camp is
several miles outside of town near Kita-
Ku," Sakusha explains.

"I know where the American camp is;
it will take me most of the day for the
trip. Now that we have rice and flour
make sure everyone has plenty to eat."
Gahou instructed Sakusha.

Gahou starts her long walk on rough roads and poor footwear for the trip on her feet.

Sakusha, with the other geishas and trainees, works together to prepare the day's meal. Rice is a regular part of the house, but flour is a luxury. They make noodles and rice in abundance.

Gahou's walk begins to take its toll on her feet, the traditional footwear a geta are fine for short walks, but miles on the war-torn road become painful and raw on her feet.

It's hours later when Gahou arrives at the sentry post of the camp. "Can I help you?" the guard asked her. Gahou's grasp of the English language was limited to what she heard from her conversation with Sakusha.

"Major. Miru Major! Miru Major!" shouts Gahou. The guard stared at Gahou, confused for a moment; the only word he understood was Major.

Reaching for his radio he calls for Major Star to come to the sentry post.

"Private, what's the problem?" Major Star addresses the guard. "It's this woman, Sir. All I understand from her is the word, Major." "Let me speak to her." To the Major Star's surprise, it's the angry woman he met at Sakusha's home.

"Can I help you?" Star asked in Japanese. Gahou bows to the Major. "I am here to apologize for my behavior. I hope you can forgive me."

Star bows, noticing the faint red stain bleeding through the cloth covering Gahou's feet.

"There is no need to apologize. My name is Major Star, and you are?" "Forgive me; my name is Namori Gahou." "Miss Gahou, follow me, please. Private, send the nurse to my tent."

"Where are you taking me, Major-san?" Gahou asked. "Before I drive you back home, I want the nurse to tend to your feet." "You do not have to do that. I am fine." "Since you came to apologize, I will accept if you let me tend to your feet." Gahou nods in agreement.

Finished with the nurse tending to Gahou's feet, Major star turns his attention to Gahou.

"Now that your feet are better, you should not have walked here to apologize. You would have seen me near your home in a few weeks. So many buildings are dangerously unstable, as the young woman I found discovered.

I gave you the rice and flour should help for a week or two. I didn't give much thought to vegetables. When I take you home, you will have some to add to your meals." Star tells Gahou.

"Why are you helping us?" Gahou asked. "I am a soldier; during the war, my duty was to defeat the enemy. The war over, it's my duty to protect and help rebuild your country. Let's get you home before it gets too dark." Major Star tells Gahou.

"Sir, your jeep is ready," Kazinski says. "Get in; you're driving," Star tells his sergeant. "Where to, Sir?" asked Sergeant Kazinski. "Do you remember this woman?" says Star as he steps away from Gahou. "Isn't she that crazy lady where we dropped off that other woman?" Kazinski asked. "The one and only, but much calmer. " "O.k., Sir," replies Kazinski.

Arriving at Gahou's home, she is surprised, there are children lined up in front of the door of her home.

"Sayori, why are all these children here?" Gahou asked. "Gahou-san, it started when we made too much rice and noodles. Not wanting it to spoil, we started feeding the children on the street. before we knew it, there were dozens of children looking for food."

Gahou lowers her head, thinking that their supplies of rice and flour will be gone soon.

Staring at Gahou's distressed expression, Major Star comes up with an idea for the women of the geisha house and the children.

"Miss Gahou, the war must have put a drastic halt to your style of life. As your country's economy starts to return, clientele will return as well.

I have a proposition that will benefit your house and the neighborhood." Major Star says. "What is it that you want?" replied Gahou.

"I will supply you with food not only for your house but enough to help the children. I heard that your women have to train many hours to become geisha. Do you think you could include feeding the children one hot meal twice a week?" Star suggested to Gahou.

"You would do that for us?" Gahou says. "If you are too busy, you can forget about it," says Star. "No! "We have time. I'm surprised you offered." says Gahou. "Since we are in agreement, I will deliver the first shipment tomorrow. First, I'll give you a hand with these vegetables." "Please do not. I will have my students bring them in. I want you and your sergeant to stay long enough for us to cook you a meal." We would be honored." Major Star replies.

"Sakusha Chisota, I want you to gather everyone outside for announcement," Gahou tells her.

chapter five

Curiosity

"Everyone is present, Gahou-san," Sakusha says. "I want everyone to listen to what I have to say. Starting soon, part of your training will incorporate cooking two meals a week for the children. If you are worried about where the food will come from, you can thank Major Star-san. He has arranged regular supplies delivered to us."

The women of the geisha house bow showing their thanks, Sakusha's eyes, unlike the other women, remain focused on the Major.

"Sergeant Kazinski, we have been invited to dinner. Remove your boots before you enter their home. It's common courtesy to do so in Japan." Star tells his sergeant.

With the vegetables, the Major and his sergeant have rice a bowl of udon noodles in vegetable broth with the occasional stares from the house's women.

On return to the camp, Major Star calls for Capitan Soyu. "You called for me, Major Star." "Yes. Tomorrow I want you to ride with the supplies delivered to Miss Gahou's home. She has agreed to cook meals twice a week for the children and whoever is in need.

Business is nonexistent for those women at the moment, and they are willing to help feed some of the starving. So please make a list of foods they can cook for the masses. Throw in several creates of military rations as well.

If you have any questions, I will be nearby with the engineer assessing the buildings that need removing so no one else gets hurt." "Sir, may I ask you a question?" Capitan Soyu asked. "Please do." "Why are you doing this?" Soyu asked. " Your rice harvest is a long way off. Mass starvation brings on disease not only to your people but mine.

These food shipments will continue at least to the next rice harvest. I will depend more on you as time goes on, not just with food but with sickness. I saw bodies that needed to be buried. I'm not foolish believing that plague will skip Kyoto. When it happens, you and I have to keep it under control.

It can supply tents for hospitals and materials, but doctors and nurses will be your job to find." Star explains. "I understand, Sir." Capitan Soyu says as he salutes.

The following day two trucks stop in front of Gahou's home. Gahou greets Capitan Soyu and ten men as they exit the back of the truck.

"Good morning," says Gahou. Capitan Soyu replies. Good morning. I have a truck filled with this food. Where do you wish these men to put it?" "You hand them to these women. They know where they belong." Gahou turns to her home. You would swear she was a drill sergeant from her next statements. "Get out here; you excuse for sluts! It's time you earned Major Star-sans generosity!"

Twenty women from their teens to late fifties rush from the house. "Capitan Soyu, have the Americans give each of my girls something to carry," Gahou instructs Soyu.

"Are you sure? Some of these grain sacks are heavy." Soyu tells Gahou.

"Do not worry about my girls. They are tougher than they look," states Gahou.

One by one, the women carried the supplies into the house. The heavy sacks of rice and flour did not pose a problem for the women. The only help they asked the Americans was to lift them onto their backs. The women slightly hunched over, carrying the grain sacks without difficulty.

In between loads, Sakusha walks over to Capitan Soyu. "Where is Major Star-san?" she asked. "The Major is where he found you unconscious. He is inspecting the damaged buildings that need tearing down, so no one like you wanders into dangerous areas."

Soyu's statement rubs Sakusha's nerves. She did not appreciate the captain's insinuation.

Sakusha continues helping unload the supplies until Gahou bows to Capitan Soyu and the American soldiers, thanking them for the food and help.

While Gahou is distracted, thanking the captain, Sakusha sneaks away from the house.

Major Star is with the officer in charge of the engineers, pointing out some of the buildings that need demolishing.

"Lieutenant Marst, I want these two buildings completely taken down. Can you do it without damaging the buildings adjacent to them?" Major Star asked.

"We can do it, Sir, with a controlled charge." "I want you to inform me when you do. I'll evacuate any locals from the area, so nobody gets hurt." "How about the ruble when we finish blasting?" Lieutenant Marst inquired. "Leave it. My job is to make sure it doesn't fall on someone. The locals will scavenge through the debris for anything useful." Major Star tells the lieutenant.

Major Star catches a familiar sight in the same alleyway where he found Sakusha, from the corner of his eye.

Walking into the alley, Star shouts. "I can see you! Miss Chitosa, you should have learned the first time walking between these buildings. If you want your clothes removed again, you can stay where you are or follow me to the jeep."

The Major helps Sakusha make her way through the rubble to his jeep.

"Why are you here? Shouldn't you be helping the other women with the food I sent?" the Major asked Shakusha.

"The food is stored away. I left the house to see what you were doing." Sakusha says. "I'm making sure people like you do not get hurt.

I cannot take you back to your home now; I have work to do. You can stay with me if you want. When I have finished, I'll drive you home." Star tells Sakusha.

When the Major finished mapping out the damaged buildings that needed tearing down, he and Sakusha start driving back to the geisha house.

"You know Miss Gahou is going to be angry at you for disappearing again," Star says. "She will not. It is my personal day. I am allowed one every month." "We shall see. I have a feeling you're supposed to let her know where you will be going." Star states. "Gahou-san does not have to know where I have been. You can agree to what I say to her."

The Major stays silent on replying to Sakusha's suggestion.

Upon arrival at the geisha's house, Gahou is outside with a distressed look on her face.

"Sakusha, where have you been?" Gahou demanded. "I was with Major Star-san," she replies.

"Is that true, Major Star-san?" Gahou asked him. "It is, but I recommend Miss Sakusha should have more training on discipline.

I discovered her wandering around the same place where I found her the first time." suggested the Major. "What! Do not tell her that! It is a lie!" Sakusha insisted.

"Miss Gahou, telling lies is not part of a geisha's training." says the Major. "That is correct. Hard work will make sure she thinks twice about stretching the truth." Gahou tells the Major. "I wish you luck, Miss Gahou." the Major says as he rides away. "I will not forget this!" Sakusha shouts.

Gahou grabs Sakusha by her ear, dragging her to the house.

chapter six

Signs

The women of the geisha house and Major Star begin their daily routines. Adding to their strict practices, feeding the starving children leaves little time for relaxation for Sakusha and the other women.

Ensuring the surrounding areas are cleared of people, Major Star, and Capitan Soyu begin blasting.

Gahou becomes disturbed when she begins hearing explosions near her home. "Does anyone know what is happening?" Calls out Gahou. The only one who knows is Sakusha since she was with Major

Star instructing his engineers which buildings he will blast.

Sakusha replies. "I do. The Americans are destroying the buildings that are too damaged to be rebuilt. If you wish me to show you where they are, I can." "You are going nowhere. Your next day for personal time is next month.

It should not be difficult finding where Major Star-san is; I need only to follow the explosions. Unlike you, I will use the roads, not the alleys."

Gahou had no intention of visiting the Major; busy with their duties, Gahou intended to tidy up the grounds in front of her home.

Help feeding the children is lovely, but the word of the women having large amounts of food stored in their building gets noticed by the seedy population of Kyoto.

"Gahou sees a man watching her from a distance. She does not have to guess who he represents.

Gahou goes back into the house, giving instructions to the women to secure the home and not to venture out of the house alone.

Leaving the women with instructions, Gahou starts walking towards the blasting until she sees Capitan Soyu in the distance.

"Capitan Soyu! Capitan Soyu!" Gahou cries outs. Gahou was lucky she called out between the blast, or Soyu would not have stopped her from walking towards the next blast area.

"Miss Gahou, it is dangerous here. Is there a reason for you to be in this area?" Capitan Soyu asked her.

"Yes. I wish to speak to Major Star-san. Is her here?" "No. He left a few minutes ago for the camp." Soyu informs Gahou. "If he is not here, could you give this letter to the Major, please?" "Is it important?" Capitan Soyu asked. "It could be," replies Gahou. "Then I will make certain that he receives it. First, I need to have you escorted away from this area. You have my word the Major will get your letter." Capitan Soyu assures Gahou.

Capitan Soyu returned to the camp to give his report on the blasting and Gahou's letter.

"What's this?" Major Star asked. "Miss Gahou-san was looking for you at the blast site. She gave this to me to pass on to you. She said it could have some importance." Capitan Soyu tells Star. "If Miss

Gahou said it could be important, let's take a look at it," says Star.

Opening the letter gives the Major cause to smile. " I can speak your language, but my reading skills are nonexistent. Could you read this for me, please?"

Capitan Soyu reads the letter, knowing well the subject matter is not to be taken likely.

"Sir, it seems your generosity towards the geisha and the children have also attracted a less scrupulous of my people.

The yakuza are watching the geisha house." Capitan Soyu informs the Major.

"Who are the Yakuza?" Star asked. "They are an underground criminal organization who are very dangerous. If they are interested in the food and supplies Gahou has in her home; it will not be long before they attempt to seize them for themselves to eat or sell." Capitan Soyu says.

"That could be a problem. Losing the geisha's food is not the issue, it can be replaced. Those women may be in danger is the problem.

Is there a way to get the local police to patrol Gahou's home more often?" Star asked.

"I could, but many of the people on the police force are yakuza. Their loyalty is somewhat questionable." Capitan Soyu points out. "I see. If you request additional patrols, I will add extra soldiers and have them carry radios to contact the camp in case of trouble. The quicker I know there's trouble, the quicker we can react.

Tomorrow when we resume tearing down buildings, stop by Gahou's home and inform her what we are going to do about her problem."

Yakuza

The stress of the unwanted notoriety the geisha house has acquired shows in Namori Gahou's expression. It has been two days since she asked Major Star for help.

"Gahou-san, are you ill?" Sayori Saya one of the maiko's asked her. "I am fine. Why do you ask?" replied Gahou. "Your face says otherwise. Is there a problem?" Saya asked her. "I am fine. If my face has this look, it is because I have to keep you and the other women of this house out of trouble."

Gahou, here's the sound of a jeep driving up to her home. She is relieved to see Captain Soyu walking down her walkway. "Capitan Soyu, do you have some news for me?" Gahou asked.

"I have Gahou-san. Is there someplace where we can speak?" Capitan Soyu asked. "Please come in. I have a spare room where we can speak in private," says Gahou.

"Gahou-san, this is what Major Star recommended about your situation; Not only will we have the police make themselves more visible around your home, there will be additional soldiers with radios patrolling the area. If anyone tries to harm you and the ladies, the Major can send help quickly."

"Please, thank Major Star-san for helping us. The presence of the police and soldiers should keep the Yakuza away." Gahou says.

"Do not become too relaxed. You still should pay attention to your surroundings. If anything or anyone is not where it should be, send someone

to inform one of the American soldiers."
Soyu tells Gahou.

The following two weeks, she pays close attention to the local police's time as they walk by her home, when feeding the masses.

Children, elderly and starving families are lining up for their well-appreciated meals outside the geisha house. The women of Gahou's home are hard at work preparing to serve the masses.

Gahou surveys the crowd, stepping outside, noticing the lack of police presence. She was not too concerned because she could have easily missed seeing the police officer on his patrol while cooking.

Feeding the crowd often takes two to three hours before ruining out of food. Today is no different; the last person in line is an orphan little girl named Sakura Nago, a tiny child no more than seven years of age.

Sakura would show up for food early, but she was last in line today.

"Hello Sakura, you're late today. Did something happen?" Gahou asked her. The shy little girl pointed at her knee. "I see. After you eat, I will put a bandage on it so that it will get better," says Gahou.

Sakura enjoys her meal; Gahou becomes suspicious, she has not seen the police officer all day. What is more disturbing are the expressions on the faces of the locals who walk past.

Gahou realizes she and the other women are in danger. If she sends one of the house's women for help, it would be putting their lives in more danger.

"Sakura, how would you like to live here from now on?" An orphan child walking away will not attract unwanted attention. "I can?" Sakura replies. "Yes, if you go and find one of the American soldiers and ask him to call Major-san.

Tell him bad men are here, Yakuza. He will understand." Gahou tells her.

Sakura scurries away, searching for an American soldier; Gahou returns to the house. " Sayori, Sakusha gather everyone; I have an important announcement," Gahou tells them. In a few minutes, everyone is waiting for Gahou's announcement.

"Listen to me carefully and do not panic. I want everyone to secure every door and window. We are in grave danger. The Yakuza will be here soon; It will not be a welcome visit. I have sent for help. When the Yakuza arrive, do nothing to provoke the them. Let me do the talking." Gahou instructs the women of her house.

Sakura walks down the main roads hoping to find one of the American soldiers patrolling. At an intersection ahead, Sakura finds her objective.

The adrenaline in her tiny body has Sakura running towards the soldier, tripping and tumbling to the ground. The pain from the fall has not set in because all Sakura has on her mind is a place to live if she gets help.

"American! American!" Sakura cries out. The soldier walks up to Sakura, helping her stand. "Can I help you?" the soldier asked.

Excited, Sakura explains that Gahou and the women are in danger in Japanese. "I don't know what you are saying." replies the soldier.

Remembering what Gahou told her, Sakura says in her best English. " Gahou bad men come to Major-san. Major-san come."

The soldier understands Sakura's message; he and the other men on patrol know there could be trouble.

The private keys his radio to contact the Major Star's receiver. "Major Star, come in, Major Star." " Major Star here." the reply is heard on the private's radio.

"Sir, I have a child with me. From what I can understand, Gahou is in danger, bad men coming." "Private, let the child speak on the radio," Star calls out to Capitan Soyu.

"You called Sir?" Soyu says. "Yes. Please speak to this child. There is trouble at the geisha's home.

"Slow down, tell me what has happened." Capitan Soyu tells Sakura. After listening to what the child says, Soyu looks at the Major. "It is as you feared, the local police are nowhere near, and the yakuza are at Gahou's home," Soyu tells Star. "Give me the radio. Soldier listen to me carefully. Call everyone to your location. Do not let anyone get near that house, and make sure that child remains with you until I arrive." Major Star commands. "I will, Sir." replies the private.

"Sergeant Kazinski!!!" Shouts Major Star. "Yes, Major! Is there a problem?" Kazinski asked. "There will be if you don't get a dozen well-armed men ready to move out in five minutes." 'Yes, Sir!" Kazinski replies.

"Capitan Soyu, you're coming with us as well," says Major Star. "What are you going to do?" Soyu asked." "You have it wrong thinking we'll be rushing into Gahou's home.

We plan now, so when we arrive, we implement our attack. It will be a two-prong insertion.

First, we take out the sentries. Then, you will go through the front door with Sergeant Kazinski and some men while I with the other group enter through the back of the building.

There's a window in the back of Gahou's home large enough to sneak in without getting noticed. If we're lucky, the women are hold in that room." Star explains to Capitan Soyu.

Capitan Star and his men meet with the little girl and the soldiers who patrol the area.

Through a set of binoculars, the Major observes a single guard is concealing a sword and gun outside of Gahou's home.

Major Star kneels in front of Sakura. "If I am to save Gahou-san and the women, I need your help," Star asked the child. "How can I help?" Sakura asked.

"I want you to walk up to that man crying for your mother. Can you do that?" Star asked. Sakura nods she can.

"First, I will add some dramatics," Star says, taking his pen from his pocket.

"Hold still, Sakura. I want that man to be afraid of you." Star says as he draws spots all over Sakura's face.

"Sergeant Kazinski, I want you to work your way behind that guard. When our little angel distracts him, you know what to do." Major Star tells him.

chapter eight

Stained affection

When Sergeant Kazinski is in position, Sakura walks toward the guard crying out for her mother.

At first, the guard pays little attention to Sakura's wailing. That changes when he gets a good look at her face.

"Stay away from me. You walking disease!" the guard tells Sakura. "Continuing to cry for her mother, Sakura closes her distance to the yakuza guard.

"Stay away from me, or I will kill you!" the guard warns Sakura before his mind goes dark from a rifle butt.

"All clear, Major. What do I do with this sword?" Kazinski asked. "Give it to

Capitan Soyu; it's more useful in his hands than ours.

Sergeant, give me five minutes, then rush the entrance or if you hear gunfire.

Keep in mind if anyone surrenders, do not kill them. I want prisoners." "As you say, Sir," replies Sergeant Kazinski.

Major Star's luck is holding out when he looks into the window of the back of Gahou's home; Most of the women are held hostages in one place with a guard back towards them, except for Gahou. The Major can hear her voice shouting at the assailants in the hallway.

"You could have asked for food; we were willing to share," Gahou tells the yakuza soldier. "We are not the sharing type. If we are hungry, we take." the yakuza soldier says.

Sakusha sees the Major looking in the window. Putting his finger to his lips, the Major signals her to silence as he climbs through the window; the

Major's sight never leaving the back of the guard.

Halfway through the window, the Major's luck runs out, with the guard turning when he hears sounds from the window.

Before the guard could raise his pistol, the Majors 45 fired several rounds. More guards rush to the back room; then, gunfire at the house entrance, confusing the yakuza.

There is gunfire and shouting throughout the house, with soldiers leaping through the window and Major Star directing them as they make their way from room to room.

It takes a few minutes before the ladies, and the house are secure. "Sergeant Kazinski, report!" Major Star calls out. "House is secure Major," Kazinski replies. "Miss Gahou, is she injured?" Star asked. "I am fine, Star-san. How about my women?" Gahou asked. "They are scared but fine." says the Major.

"Sergeant Kazinski, what did we take for injuries?" Major Star asked. "We were lucky. No deaths, a few minor injuries. Including the one, you killed three dead yakuza and three taken alive." reported Kazinski.

Take our prisoners outside; I'll deal with them in a few minutes." "Yes, Major," replies Sergeant Kazinski.

Major Star turns to make sure the women in the room are not injured; he does see blood on Sakusha's face and clothes.

"Miss Sakusha, are you hurt?" Star asked her. "No," she replies. "There's blood on your face and clothes. Let me clean it."

Star uses his handkerchief to wipe away the blood spatter on Sakusha's face. Sakusha's eyes are fixed upon Stars' face as he cleans her face.

"I cleaned what I could from your clothes; I am afraid the blood will stain unless you wash it in cold water before it dries." Major Star suggested to Sakusha. "Thank you; I will." "I have to tend to my prisoners; I'm glad you are not hurt," says Major Star.

"Capitan Soyu, I need to discuss the fate of these prisoners with you, and will the yakuza retaliate." Major Star asked.

"I would not put past for the yakuza to take revenge," Soyu says.

"If they do, the women may not be so lucky. I have an idea. I'll release one of the prisoners with a message to meet with the local boss. The other two will remain in our custody depending on the outcome of the meeting." Star tells Capitan Soyu.

"Major Star-san, thank you for coming to our rescue," Gahou says. "Do not thank me; Sakura was the one who called me." Major Star says. "Yes, I know. She has a new home, with many older sisters to pamper her." Gahou tells Major Star.

Sakusha walks up to the Major; she tugs on his shirt to get his attention. "Is there something I can help you with?" asked the Major.

" I would like to ask a favor of you," Sakusha asked. "If I can grant it, please ask." replies the Major.

"I am allowed one day a month for a personal time. Can I spend it with you?'

Star is surprised by Sakusha's request. He looks to Gahou. "Is she permitted to spend time with me? I am not familiar with your rules and culture regarding geisha." Major Star asked Gahou.

"It is her day. She can do whatever she wants. At least with you, she will not get into trouble." states Gahou.

"Miss Sakusha Chisato, you give me the day, and I will pick you up here. I sure we can find something to do in Kyoto." Major Star says.

"My next personal day is the fifteenth of next month," Sakusha tells Major Star. "I will see you then or earlier if I am in the neighborhood. Thank you for considering me worthy of sharing your time Miss Chitosa."

chapter nine

Negotiations

"Sir, what did you write on that letter you gave to the yakuza soldier?" Capitan Soyu asked. "I requested to meet with his boss. I'm sure neither of us want another war. If the meeting is agreed upon, we'll meet outside Gahou's home.

In the meantime, I have a report to send to my superior, that might raise an eyebrow." Major Star says.

Major Star's report reaches General Bast's eyes with some surprise. The General decides to pay a visit to the Major post.

The General's car arrives at the front entrance. The guard salutes. Returning his salute General Bast speaks to the sentry. "Advise your commander that I'm paying him a visit." "Yes, Sir!" shouts the guard.

Sergeant Kazinski's phone rings. He receives the sentry's message of General Bast's arrival.

"Sir, General Bast is on his way here, he just entered the front gate." Kazinski informs the Major.

"He's here because of my last report. When the General arrives, post guards around my office, let no one enter." Major Star ordered his Sergeant.

The Major stands at attention with a lump in his throat as General Bast enters the room. "At ease Major. I'm here to share some of that single malt scotch you have on your desk and discuss your last report that was so interesting to read." General Bast says.

Nervously Star waits for the General to finish his drink.

"Much better. I've seen your requisition for two truckload of military rations. What are you planning to do with them?. Before you answer that question, talk to me about the geisha's you're helping." the General inquired.

"Sir, we are allowed to provide humanitarian aid. I found one of the geisha's injured by chance. When I returned her home, it gave me the perfect opportunity to use them as a soup kitchen for the hungry children.

Doing so gave me a foothold on establishing some of the local's trust. Americans are not well liked for some reason." jokingly Major Star says.

"Now explain the trucks fill with rations," states General Bast.

"Sir, using the geisha's did get the attention of the local criminal organization. The yakuza wanted the supplies I gave to the geishas. So they forced me to intervene.

We had some none fatal injuries on our part; the yakuza's lost three of their people.

I have no wish to get into another war with anyone. I need the trucks of food to make a deal with the yakuza. It will not be a payoff. I want to offer the food for a condition to work with the community on clearing up the rubble and help keep the looting down." Star explains.

"How are you going to do that?" General Bast asked. "The yakuza may be criminals but betting they are patriotic. That's the angle I'm going to pitch to them." the Major explains to General Bast.

"I will allow your requisition of the rations to go through with the condition of weekly reports on the yakuza's involvement in Kyoto. If your plan works, I can use it in other locations in Japan. I'll be looking for your reports. I can't stay long, I have other camps to inspect." states General Bast as he leaves.

Sergeant Kazinski sticks his head in his Major's office when General Bast leaves. "How was your talk with the General?" Kazinski asked. "Better than I thought; he's allowing me to make a deal with the yakuza. The General wants weekly progress reports on Kyoto and the assistance programs I have ongoing." Major Star explains.

"That sounds like a lot of paperwork, Sir." Sergeant Kazinski comments. "It will be." says Star.

A week passes when a man walks up to the sentry at the Army camp. "Yes, can I help you?" the guard asked. "This is for you commanding office." says the man, then walks away.

The guard picks up his radio. "Sergeant Kazinski." "Yes, what is it?" Kazinski replies. "Someone handed me a letter to give to the Major." the sentry tells him." "Hold on to it. I will be right there. The Major has been waiting for that letter." Kazinski tells the guard.

"Major, someone just delivered a message to the sentry for you. I'm on my way to get it." Sergeant Kazinski informs him.

"Good. Let's hope the yakuza want to talk." says Star.

Sergeant Kazinski hurries to the guard post and back. "Here it is, Sir." Sergeant Kazinski says, breathing heavy.

The Major is relieved, the letter is in English, and the yakuza agree to meet.

"Is it good news, Sir?" Kazinski asked. "So far, it is. They have agreed to meet with us in front of Gahou's home in two days. Also, they will allow only me and one other soldier as an escort. Don't get your hopes up. I need someone who understands the language. Capitan Soyu will be tagging along." Major Star tells his Sergeant.

The day arrives, Major Star and Capitan Soyu are standing outside Gahou's home. "I wonder if the yakuza boss changed his mind? I don't see him." Major Star says to Soyu.

Gahou opens her door, signaling to the Major to enter. "Who you are waiting for is in here. I have reserved a room for your meeting. The leader of the yakuza explained his circumstances. I suggested that he should use one of the rooms for his meeting."Gahou explains to Major Star.

Entering the room, Major Star and Capitan Soyu greet the yakuza boss and his lieutenant, who stand with a bow and introduction.

"I am Major Star, and this is Capitan Soyu; thank you for agreeing to meet," says Star.

"I am Tokato Moshitka, and this Saito, we are here to discuss your proposition."

"How well is your English?" Major Star asked Moshitoka. "I speak and understand it well," Yoshitaka tells the Major.

"Moshitoka-san, a war between you and the American army will not go well for you or my men and the ladies of this house. I wish to ask you a question. Are you patriotic?" says the Major.

"What kind of question is that.?" Yoshitaka inquired. "In every country, there are criminal organizations. Believe it or not, they are very loyal to their country. So I am asking you are loyal to yours?" Major Star says to Moshitka.

Staring into the Major's eyes, Moshitoka can tell the Major is serious about the question. "I am very loyal to my country," Yoshitaka replies.

"That is what I was hoping to hear. I want to hire your services." Major Star asked.

Morishita is surprised by Major Star's request. "The U.S military is not ones to ask someone like my organization to kill," Morishita says. "I'm not asking you to harm anyone. It's the opposite. You know everyone in Kyoto and have the human resources to help rebuild it.

I want your people to help keep the crime rate down and help the homeless rebuild or find homes for them for one year." requested the Major. "You are asking much from me. What do you have to offer as payment?" Yoshitaka inquired.

"Four tons of military rations to do what you wish with them." Major Star offered.

"Four tons! It will take several trucks to move that much merchandise," says Moshitoka tells the Major. "I'll have it delivered to any location you wish.

Do I have your word you will help your people?" Major Star asked Moshitoka.

The head of the yakuza bows. "I will do as you ask," says Morishitoka. Major Star bows. "Your word is good enough for me. All I need to know is, where do you want it delivered?"

chapter ten

The fifteenth

Tokato Morishitoka kept his word. The once-feared yakuza are now respected and welcomed by the local population of Kyoto.

Streets are clear of rubble, with many homeless having their homes rebuilt or finding shelters for the homeless.

Life in Kyoto became tolerable; starvation and disease were still the main problems. At the geisha's home, one very upbeat geisha is waiting for someone to stop by to pick her up.

"Chisato-san, here is a list the other women and I want when you visit the city with Major Star-san." Yuki Suzuhito says to Sakusha. "How come I have to look for these items? Why cannot the others search for them on their day?" Sakusha tells Yuki.

"The Major-san has his vehicle, and he may know where to find some of nice smelling soaps or shampoo," Yuki says.

"Some of these items we are not supposed to have. If Gahou finds out you have them, she will take them away," says Sakusha. "We did not ask for those; it was Gahou," Yuki says. "O.k. I will do what I can." Sakusha says.

The sound of a jeep ends the conversation between Yuki and Sakusha. "I have to go; I do not wish for Major Star-san to wait for me."

Sakusha's heart pounds with excitement as she opens the door to meet the Major.

There is a new experience; Entranced, the Major's eyes feast on Sakusha. Her hair tied back in a beautiful kimono adds a gentle smile to Major Star's war wary face.

Sakusha is so excited when she attempts to speak to the Major, her voice cracks up, making her sound like a mouse, causing her and the Major's face to blush.

The Major watches as Sakusha struggles to climb in the jeep, the kimono she wears restricts her legs. Major Star steps out of the jeep, walking around to Sakusha.

"Miss Chisato-san, I do not want you to panic; I am going to help you get in the jeep." Major Star says.

With one arm supporting her back, Major Star places the other arm on the back of Sakusha's legs, lifting her into the jeep's front seat.

Now that the Major and Sakusha are in the jeep, Star looks at his passenger's beet-red face. "Is there any place you would like to visit? I see you are holding something in your hand." Star says. It takes a moment for

Sakusha to regain her composer before replying.

"Oh, this is nothing. The other women of the house wish take advantage of you for their personal reasons. Please disregard this paper; I will throw it away." Sakusha tells Star.

"Please do not discard it. May I see it?" Major Star asked. Sakusha hands the notepaper to the Major. "Can you read this to me? I cannot read Japanese.

I can tell that most of the women are asking for the same thing. There are one or two different items that are different." Major Star says.

"You are correct; most of the women are requesting scented soap and shampoo for their hair. This woman is asking for a hairpiece; this one wants makeup." Sakusha points out. "What does this woman want?" Star points to the list. " She wants American nylon stockings." "Would that be you wanting the nylons?" Star asked Sakusha. "It is not I who asked for the stockings. That is Gahou -sans request."

"That is a surprise. I would not have thought Gahou-san wanted Nylons." Star says.

"It surprised us all. American clothing is forbidden to wear." Sakusha explains to Star. "No matter where you're from, a woman is still a woman." Major Star states.

Hold on to that list; we might find what those women want in Tokyo. I know someone who could help us find what those ladies need." says Star.

"We are going to Tokyo?" Sakusha asked, surprised. "If you do not want to go, we can remain in Kyoto if you wish?" "No! I would love to visit Tokyo." Sakusha blurts out.

The drive to Tokyo is slow; many of the roads are sad due to bombings from the war. There are still many signs of death and starvation, which upsets Sakusha. One in particular is very upsetting. A mother standing outside her burnt home, grieving over her dead children, using her bare hands to dig their graves.

A hardened soldier like Major Star is finding it difficult to watch. "Miss Chisato-san, I have a shovel in the jeep. Speak to a woman while digging their graves." the Major says, stopping the jeep.

Every shovel full of dirt Major Star fights back the tears knowing the mother of these five-year-old twins' grief is unbearable.

Major Star could have dug one grave for both children; he did not. The children's mother deserved more than a grave; Major Star used parts of the mother's burnt home to make a small make-shift shrine.

The mother of the children held no grudge against the Major. Whatever anger she had for the death of her children was replaced with gratitude by Major Star's action.

"Chisato-san ask the woman if she has someplace to live." Major Star requested.

Sakusha spoke to the woman, asking if she had any relatives or husbands. The Major can tell by the woman's nodding of her head she had no one.

"Chisato-san, do you think Gahou-san could house her for a day or two?" "What do you have in mind, Major Star - san?" Sakusha asked.

"I can offer her a job as my maid. I am a slob. I could use help keeping my office and sleeping quarters clean. She will have a place to sleep, meals and a salary. I need a couple of days to set up her living quarters."

Sakusha explains the Major's proposal to the woman. Through the tear-stained and dirt-covered face, a ray of hope shines on the woman's face.

Major Star bows to the woman. "I am Major Frank Star, and you are?" the Major asked. Bowing, the woman introduces herself. "I am Sakano Okina. I wish to accept your offer." "If you wish, you can continue to grieve. I can pick you up when I return from Tokyo." suggested the Major.

"Major Frank Star-san I will always grieve for my children. I am grateful for you doing more than my people would have done to help. I have nothing here to keep me. I am your servant." says Sakano.

With the two ladies as passengers, Major Star destination in Tokyo is the leading distribution warehouse of the American forces.

"First Sergeant Wise, how's peace fitting in with your social life?" Major Star says. "Major! Are you here? I thought you were in charge of Kyoto's district." replies Wise.

"I am. I'm here to ask for a favor." Major Star says. "If I can, sure," replies First Sergeant Wise.

These two ladies need your help. This one is Sakusha Chisato. She and other women she lives with are feeding the homeless children using with Army's help. She has a list of items they have requested. Most of the things are fancy-smelling soaps and shampoo.

You were always good at procuring hard-to-find products. I would appreciate it if you help Sakusha with her shopping list." Major Star asked. "I think I can help her. If don't have it; I can get it," states Wise.

This other woman is Sakano Okina. She will be my maid at the camp. Is there somewhere for her to shower?" the Major asked.

"There is a shower in the back. Does the woman need anything?" First Sergeant Wise asked. "She could use some clothes and personal soaps and shampoo." requested the Major. "Leave it to me, Sir. You can show Miss Okina to the shower while Miss Chisato and I do some shopping," says First Sergeant Wise.

chapter eleven

Maid service

"Okina-san, sorry for the green clothing; when we return to Kyoto, I will search for more fitting clothes for you to wear." Major Star says.

"Do not worry Major Star-san about my clothes. I am happy washing with the fragrance soap. I have not smelled this nice in a long time." replies Okina.

"You're very quiet, Sakusha. I thought you would be happy finding everything and more that was on the list," says Star. "I am happy, maybe a little tired from the trip," Sakusha says.

Sakano is much older and has more experience in life than Sakusha; she recognizes Sakusha's plight. "Major Star-san is there someplace you can stop. I need to relieve myself." Sakano asked. "I am not sure where I can stop; most homes are destroyed in this area," Star tells Sakano.

"Up ahead, there is a burnt home; behind it, I can see the small building is untouched. That should be the toilet. I am certain Sakusha must need to use the toilet as well." Sakano says.

Sakusha looks at Sakano strangely from her statement. Sakano gently nods, signaling that Sakusha needs to follow her. "Yes, I need to use the toilet," Sakusha tells the Major.

Pulling over, Star reaches into his pouch. "Before you go you might need this." the Major says, handing Sakano a roll of toilet paper. "What is this?" Sakano asked. "One of the luxuries of life, use it to wipe yourself." states the Major.

The two ladies walk to the outhouse. "Sakano, why did you want me to follow you?" Sakusha asked her.

"Now that we are out of the American Major's sight, I can speak to you.

I can see it on your face." "What? Do I have the plague?" Sakusha says with panic.

"Not that silly girl. You have feelings for the American Major, and you are worried that he may like me and me likewise.

I am grateful for what Major Star is doing to help me. I have no interest in having a relationship with him. In the little time I have known him, I can tell he is genuine about his intentions. I am his servant and, in time, his friend.

You are falling in love with him; I wish you luck and happiness.

It will be a difficult journey for you. Your mannerisms tell me you are geisha. Am I correct?" Sakano asked.

"I am Maiko," replies Sakusha. "All the same, you are a commodity of Japan. Even if you take the American Major as your dana, you will be ostracised.

Major Star-san recognizes your beauty and probably wishes to spend more time with you, but his situation is no different than yours.

Major Star-san is a high-ranking American officer; he must be cautious about getting involved with a geisha.

The Major seems to be very level-headed. When you are ready, discuss your feelings with him. I am sure he will understand. Now I need to go to the toilet. I had to go." Sakano tells Sakusha.

Returning to the jeep, Star sees a noticeable difference in Sakusha's smile. "You look relieved." says the Major. "I am. I relieved myself of a heavy burden." Sakusha says.

The rest of the way to Kyoto, Major Star ponders Sakusha's statement, thinking how the Japanese passionately describe the relief of taking a dump.

Several women are outside waiting for the Major's jeep as he arrives at Gahou's house.

How was your day, Major-san?" Gahou greets him. "I picked up a passenger." Major Star says. "I see. Who is she?" Gahou inquired. "Sakano Okina, this is Namori Gahou. She is the head of the house." Star says.

The two women bow with a pleasant greeting. "Miss Gahou, I would like to ask a favor from you, if possible." Major Star says.

"Please ask. I do not know if I can grant it." Gahou replies. "I have hired Okina-san as my servant. It will take me two days to prepare her living quarters at the camp. I was hoping she could stay with you for those two days." Major Star explains.

"I will be happy to house Okina-san until you are ready to receive her. You have done so much for us; it will be a pleasure to help you," says Gahou.

"Thank you." says the Major. "No, thank you. You have made many women of this house very happy, including me. I have wanted nylon stockings for a long time.

It would be best if you did not worry about her clothing. I will make sure that Okina-san has the appropriate clothes to wear as your servant." "Gahou-san, you are an angel," says Star.

Climbing back into his jeep, someone rushes up to him before driving away.

"Major Star-san, must you leave so soon?' Sakusha asked him. "I am needed back at the camp. I will return in two days to pick up, Okina-san. On your next personal day, would you like if we went on a picnic?" Major Star says. Sakusha's face glows with joy and excitement, not because of the picnic but the Major is asking her.

Bowing, Sakusha replies. "I would be delighted to go on a picnic with you, Star-san. "I need to go. I will look forward to next month," says Star.

Back in his office, Major Star ponders where Sakano will be sleeping. She can't sleep in the building he's living in, which could lead to too many rumors and temptation.

"Sergeant Kazinski!" calls out the Major. "You called Sir?" Kazinski says. "Yes. I have a dilemma. I will have a woman working for me as a maid in two days. Her name is Sakano Okina. Is there someplace we can house her that is not too far from my quarters?" Star asked.

"There is a small building she could live in, but it's on the opposite side of the camp." Sergeant Kazinski stated.

"Can it be moved? We have plenty of excavating equipment." Major Star asked. "I think it can." Sergeant Kazinski says. "Make it happen. Move it close enough to my quarters where the woman will feel safe. There is plenty of hatred towards the Japanese in my command; keeping Mrs. Okina close but not too close will keep the malcontents away.

Did I miss anything while I was away?" Major Star asked. "Not much. A couple of the men came down with some bug. The medic is keeping them in bed for a couple of days." Sergeant Kazinski informs him.

"Sergeant, once you have the house moved, furnish it with a cot, a trunk to store her clothes, and see if you can find a mirror to hang on a wall." Yes Sir." Kazinski says, saluting.

It has come time for the major to pick up Sakano. Gahou greets Star at his jeep. Good morning Star-san." "Good morning Gahou-san. Is Okina-san ready for her first day on the job?" asked the Major.

"See for yourself. Okina-san, you can come out," says Gahou.

The Major sees a noticeable difference in Sakano. "Proper clothing, nothing too colorful to stand out. As a servant, she must not be the center of attention. Okina-san has extra clothing. Everyone in the house donated a piece of clothing." Gahou explains.

"That is wonderful. Where is Sakusha? I would have thought she would want to talk to me." the Major inquired.

"She is restricted to the house. Sakusha has been neglecting her studies. Her tea ceremony is atrocious with a lackluster ikebana arrangement. If she does not improve, she will lose her personal day." Gahou tells Major Star.

"Gahou-san, may I make a suggestion?" Sakano asked. "Please do if it will help Sakusha's studies. "Maybe, Sakusha needs to be inspired.

Before Sakusha's next personal day, test her by having her perform the tea ceremony and ikebana correctly for Major Star-san." "I think that is a wonderful idea. How do you feel about being Sakusha's test subject?" Gahou asked the Major. "I' don't mind. When will you have the test?" Major Star asked. In two weeks. That is plenty of time for Sakusha to prepare."Gahou says.

"I will look forward to seeing her in two weeks.

Okina-san, let's get you acquainted with your new home and job.

Arriving at the camp's front gate, the sentry salutes. "Private, keep this woman's face in mind. Her name is Sakano Okina, and she has access to come and go to the camp as an employee. You will receive an updated list of people who are allowed entry by the end of the day." "Yes, Sir!" shouts the guard as he salutes.

Driving to his quarters; the Major showed Okina where she was sleeping.

"It's not fancy, but you will be dry and warm. Inside, there is a bed and a place to store your clothing." Star explains.

"Where will you live?' Sakano asked. "That building." the Major points. "May I see what I have to keep clean?" Sakano asked. "O.k."

Entering the Major's home, Sakano looks around, then turns to the Major.

"Is it too late to request you take me back to my burnt home?" Sakano says. "It 's not that bad." replies the Major.

chapter twelve

Tiny death

"Are you still angry about not letting you speak to Major Star-san?" Gahou says to Sakusha. "You will in two weeks," says Gahou. "Why two weeks? Is there something happening?" Sakusha asked.

"Yes. In two weeks, you will be performing the tea ceremony and ikebana in front of the Major. If your effort is not satisfactory, you will lose your personal day." Gahou tells Sakusha. "You cannot do that," states Sakusha. "I can, and I will, or you will leave this house.

Ask yourself, is Major Star-san worth it. I know you have feelings for him; it is time to show it in your work." Gahou tells Sakusha.

At the camp, Okina's the second day as Major Star's servant starts with having breakfast with the enlisted and other officers.

"Why do I have to eat my meal with you in this place?" Okina asked the Major. "These people need to know who you are, that's why," replies Star

Looking to the left of Major Star is an officer under his command. "Capitan." is all that the Major says. The Capitan instinctively knows what to do. Standing up, he calls out attention in a loud decisive voice.

The dozens of personnel in the mess tent stand at attention.

Star stands up. "Now that I have your attention, this woman sitting beside me will have access to the camp. She works for me and is under my command only. Do you understand!" shouts the Major. "In a roar, everyone replies they do.

"Thank you, please continue your meal," says Major Star. Okina gives the Major a scowling look. "That was not necessary." "We will discuss how necessary it is later. Let's enjoy our breakfast." Star says.

"Now that you have embarrassed me and your bedroom is clean, what else am I needed to do?" " You can tidy up my office then have the rest of the day to yourself. "If there is anything you might need personally, I can assign a driver to take you into Kyoto. The building you will live in is simple in taste. Sleeping on a cot may not be to your liking." Major Star says.

"I would like to see if I can find a tatami mat and futon sometime this week," Sakano suggested. "When you're ready to go, tell me. I will assign a driver to take you to town." Major Star tells Sakano.

Later on in the day, Sakano is in Star's office cleaning as the Major reads the daily reports. Sakano notices that Major Star is looking troubled.

"Major-san, is there something troubling you?" Sakano asked. "There is; more of my people are becoming ill. First, it was two; now, three more have a fever. We have a medic who is good with injuries but has little knowledge of diseases. So I have to contact Tokyo, asking for a doctor to diagnose the problem." Major Star says. "It could be the plague," Sakona tells the Major. "That's what I hope it's not," says Major Star.

"I have seen many sicknesses. If you allow me to look at the people, I might know what illness they have," suggested Sakano. "Follow me," says Star.

Entering the medical tent, the Major calls for the corpsman. "Sir." "How are they doing?" Major Star asked. "Not well, Sir. I wish I knew what I was dealing with." states the corpsman.

"I'm allowing Mrs. Okina to examine the men. She has some experience with diseases." Major Star informs the corpsman.

Sakano carefully examines the sick soldiers, but it does not take her long to come to a conclusion.

"Major-san, I have seen this before. I believe they have cholera." Sakona tells the Major.

Not understanding Japanese, the corpsman asked the major what Sakona told him. "Sir, what did she say?" "She thinks it's cholera. If it is, I want a quarantine tent set up. I'll contact the General advising him we may have a cholera outbreak. We need a doctor to confirm the disease." Major Star informs the corpsman.

A courier is sent to headquarters, informing them there could be a plague in Kyoto.

General Bast takes any hint of plague seriously; sending a doctor to Kyoto immediately.

"Major Star, I'm the doctor, Captain Sear. Where are the men you suspect of having cholera?" "I quarantined them away from the other personnel in a separate tent. Follow me." Star says.

It does not take long for Captain Sear to confirm Okina's diagnosis.

"Major Star, where have these men been in the last two weeks?" Captain Sear asked.

These three have been patrolling Kyoto and spending their time in the nearby town." Major Star replied.

"Where do you get your water from?" Capitan Sear asked. "We have a well on the base," Star says.

"From now on, boil all water before drinking. I am requesting lab equipment. I need you to get water samples from every well between here and in Kyoto.

Those soldiers drank water from a contaminated water supply. Also, send people out asking if any of the locals are ill. We have to narrow down which wells are contaminated and why." Captain Sear instructs Major Star.

Returning to his office, Major Star has a difficult task ahead. It will not be easy finding all the wells for testing.

"The Major calls for Captain Soyu and his servant Okina. Major Star, what has happened?" Captain Soyu asked.

"Okina, you were correct about cholera. The doctor believes the wells in and around Kyoto could be contaminated. So it's our job to find out which ones are and how they became that way.

I need to recruit the locals to get samples of every well and their location they can find.

Also, ask around if anyone is ill. If we don't find the source of cholera, there could be a lot more needless deaths.

We will pay a visit to Gahou to ask for her help. If I supply the transportation, the ladies can go house to house asking for samples of water." Major Star tells Captain Soyu.

"Sergeant Kazinski!" Star calls out. "Yes, Major?" "Get me a jeep!" with authority; Star tells his sergeant. "Yes, Sir! Where are we going?" Kazinski asked. We are going to Gahou's home." Major Star tells him.

chapter thirteen

The search

"Major Star-san, Sakusha is not ready for her trial," Gahou says. "Miss Gahou, I am not here for Sakusha. Something much more important and deadly is the reason." explains the Major.

"Please enlighten me," says Gahou. "Of the people who visit you for food, are any of them sick or missing?" Major Star asked. "Now that you mention it, I have not seen some of the regulars. What is this about?" Gahou asked the Major.

"Gahou-san, you must boil all drinking water until further notice. There is an outbreak of cholera. Some of the wells are contaminated, and I need to ask for your help." Major Star says.

"How can I help you, Major-san?" asked Gahou. "I need your women and anyone else you know to go door to door asking to take samples of the water in their wells.

A tent will be in the city to isolate and tend to the sick, also I will provide transportation for those who will help in the search. I must find where the contamination is coming from, or the death rate will spread.

I have several men sick already. See if you can locate those who are missing from your meals. I'll have them treated at the field hospital." Major Stars instructs Gahou.

"We will help. When are we to start this search?" Gahou asked. "Tomorrow. I will supply the containers to take the samples," says Star.

"Major Star-san, leave me here with Gahou-san. I will help organize the search for the people who are presumed ill, and these women need to know how to react if they come across someone who has cholera." Okina tells the Major.

"You cleaned, organized my quarters and office in a day; That's a feat in it's self. I will leave it in your hands to have everyone organized for tomorrow." Okina is told.

Okina starts by speaking to Gahou when Major Star returns to the camp.

"Gahou-san, may I speak to your ladies of the house? I need to inform them what has happened?" Okina asked her. "Please do. I will call for them," says Gahou.

Calling the house's women to come outside in a loud and commanding voice.

"Gahou, what is this time?" Sakusha and the other women asked. "As you can see, Okina -san is here. So please listen to her carefully."

"There is not much time to discuss why I am here. We have an outbreak of cholera. Tomorrow the Americans will be here with trucks. We must help them determine which wells in the area are contaminated.

Fewer people will die if we can get more people to help search. In the meantime, boil all water before using. When the people arrive for food today, inform them of the danger. Those you suspect sick have brought them here so that Major Star-san can care for them in the field hospital.

I need one person to tear up a sheet in strips to cover your nose and mouth.

I suggest you boil as much water ahead of time as you can store for those who depend on you for food."

Sakusha's frown catches Okina's attention. she whispers to her." Do not look so sad; you will see him tomorrow."

Once returned to the camp Major Star discusses the next day's operation with the doctor.

"Capitan Sear, everything will be in place tomorrow morning on collecting water samples. How are the men doing?" Major Star asked. "Not well. A few more soldiers have come down with cholera. I have requested a new wonder drug shipped to this location.

If you want good news, the water at the camp is safe. Those men who are ill drank water that the locals offered." Captain Sear explains.

"I suspected as much. Some of the people who show up at the food bank are missing. I have people searching for them as we speak.

Can I borrow the corpsman? I am setting up a field hospital to isolate the sick in Kyoto until I find a local doctor to assist." I don't need him. I have requested more nurses. They should arrive tomorrow." Captain Sear informs the Major.

"Capitan Soyu, I need you to find a doctor to help with the impending problem. I will supply what medical supplies are needed to help. Take a jeep and start looking." Major Star insisted.

Sakano Okina is a strong-minded woman with foresight on seeing the big picture with excellent organizational skills. She takes on the task with vigor on recruiting more help and locating those who have contracted cholera.

Major Star arrives at Gahou's home, knowing everyone knows what to do.

"Major-san, everyone is ready. We have plenty of volunteers to assist with the search." Okina informs him.

"That's great. You have my job much easier. I have four trucks for us to use; Three to carrier those who will attain the water samples and one to use as an ambulance for the sick." Major Star tells Okina.

"You do not have to search for those who are ill. The sick are here." Okina informs the Major. "You were busy yesterday. How many people did you find who are sick?" asked Star. "twenty, so far. I am certain there are more I have not discovered." states Okina.

"Gahou, Sakusha, I need you here for a moment," Star says. Laying out a map, Major Star explains how they will execute this search to the ladies.

"Gahou, you Sakusha and Okina-san will be in charge of each group. You will be assigned an area to start your search. There will be an enlisted with an officer with each group. Before we start, see if any of your volunteers are familiar with your search area. Doing so will make your job much easier.

Sakusha, you will be riding in my truck, Okina; you're with Sergeant Kazinski and Captain Soyu when he arrives. Okina, you're with lieutenant Bloss and his corporal. You need to instruct them where to go." Major Star informs the ladies.

Sakusha feels her heartbeat knowing she will be in the truck Star is driving, but she is also concerned why the Major is not acknowledging her.

Before the ladies go to their assigned trucks, Gahou pulls Sakusha aside, away from the crowd.

Gahou's expression is more stern than usual. "Sakusha, I need you to listen to what I have to tell you. Major-san is not here to shower you with attention, nor you to expect it.

He asked you to help, thinking you are a woman, not a child with a crush. I know Major-san enough to tell you he does not have time to try to impress you. There are too many lives at stake for him to be concerned with your insecurities. You have an essential job to do; I suggest you put your effort into saving people."

When finished with her discussion, Sakusha silently stepped into the back of the truck with the other volunteers.

Methodically, Okina, Gahou, and Sakusha went door to door with the volunteers requesting and documenting where they got the water samples. Unfortunately, it was not until dark that they completed collecting the samples.

Tired and hungry, the three ladies and those who helped collect the samples had a treat waiting for them returning at Gahou's home.

Major Star had his cooks prepare hot meals for the volunteers.

chapter fourteen

Scars

"Major-san, thank you for this food. I
will remind everyone to boil their water
before using it. How long will it take
before you find the cause of the
disease?" Gahou asked.

"I do not know. The doctor has to
check the water samples to find the
location of the contamination.

Off the subject of water: What did you
say to Sakusha? You're the only person
I can think of who could get her to be so
quiet." Major Star asked. "I reminded
her she is not riding with you to be
infatuated, but to help save lives,"
Gahou tells the Major.

"If you told her that, I should say
goodbye before I return to the base,"
says Major Star.

Calling to Sakusha. " "Miss Chisato-san, can I speak to you for a moment?" Star asked her.

"Yes, Major Star -san?" says Sakusha. "I would like to thank you for your help. It made my task much easier." Sakusha bows. "It was my pleasure helping you to help my people." "Can see your hand for a moment?" Star asked.

She is curious why the Major would ask for her hand; she does what he asks. Gently holding Sakusha's hand, the Major gently kisses it. "Thank you, and I look forward to your exams. I must return to my base. I wish you well."

Major Star leaves Sakusha standing in a haze as he walks away.

"Chitosa, Chitosa, wake up!" "Sayori Saya a maiko shouts. "Oh? Forgive me." Sakusha says. You look lost in thought. What was on your mind?" Saya asked her. "Sakusha smiles; holding her hand, she replies, " An English knight."

Days pass, Major Star waits for the results of the water samples. "Doctor Sear, how goes the search?" Major Star asked. "I have the problem area narrowed down to the Shimamoto area. Look at this map. The contamination is more prevalent around these wells and lessens as you work away. You're going to find the cause of the contaminated wells somewhere in this area." Captain Sear points out on the map.

"Thanks, doctor, I'll have people searching that area tomorrow." says the Major. "When you do find the cause, be very cautious. There are all kinds of harsh chemicals besides cholera in the contamination. It may be a dumping site. If it is, I suggest you have your gas mask handy." Captain Sear tells the Major. "Thanks for the advise, Doctor." replies the Major.

In a secluded place hidden by a small forest Major Star, a little east of Kyoto, discovers a massive waste dumping site. As Star approaches the area, Captian Soyu pulls him away, telling everyone to back away from the area. He discovered some information of the area while searching for a doctor.

"Captain Soyu, you're keeping us away. What are we walking into?" Major Star inquired.

"Sir, when I was searching for a doctor, I came across troubling information about our military. The Japanese military used this place not only to dump human waste but chemicals; the military dumped chemical and biological weapons waste was disposed of here as well."

"Shit! I want everyone to evacuate this area now! Sergeant Kazinski!" Major Star shouts. "Sir! What is it?" Kazinski asked with concern. "Sergeant, I want two dozen armed guards cordoning off this area. No one is allowed to enter unless I say so!" "Yes, Sir!" Sergeant Kazinski replies.

"Captian Soyu, you and I have to speak to the doctor and then General Bast."

An urgent message is sent to General Bast, informing him of the danger and requesting a meeting to deal with the problem.

General Bast arrives at Star's command with a contingent of officers.

"Major Star, having you in my command makes life interesting. I want to hear Captain Sear' s assessment of the dump site.

Captain Sear, how bad could it get if we do nothing?" General Bast asked.

"Sir, if this waste site is left untreated, Kyoto's water will be undrinkable in a year or two. That is the least of your worries; We'll have diseases we never heard of killing us along with the locals on a massive scale." Captain Sear explains to General Bast.

"How do we fix this?" General Bast asked Captain Sear. "General, it's going to take monumental effort. The shear size of the dump site is challenging. Everything will need to be burned, not only on the surface but also deep beneath the surface. The swamp especially. Then lime is added and mixed with what is left.

When finished, it needs to be buried in concrete away from the water supply." Doctor Sear's suggestion is staggering.

General Bast's expression is not a happy one. "Major Star, this is beyond my rank. I need to contact the man in charge. The four stars he has on his hat will give him the authority to deal with this mess and implement a suggestion I will recommend. I will contact you when I have an answer. In the meantime, do not let anyone near that place." General Bast tells the Major.

"I have it under guard as we speak. No one will get near the place until I get your o.k." Major Star assures the General.

It takes less than a week for General Bast to return with a course of action.

Major Star, you will have the materials and machines to clean the waste site; first, the General thought highly of my suggestion.

I want everyone wearing complete chemical war gear when as I walk a few people to the site." "As you say, General Bast." says the Major.

The day before cleaning up the dump site, a line of Japanese military and government officials are at the site. Escorting them are soldiers dressed in bio hazard suits and gas masks.

One of the Japanese officials looks at General Bast. "Why have we been brought here?" he asked.

"Look around; you may notice everyone dressed a certain way." replies the General. "If there is a danger that warrants protective gear, should we be wearing some?" asked the Japanese official. "Ask that military officer beside you; he is looking very nervous since he knew about this place.

The air, soil, and water from this place will kill you if you remain here too long. Am I correct?" General says, staring at the officer.

Why would you put a chemical and biological weapons waste dump site near a major city, knowing it could poison the population's water supply?

The dead animals you see lying around die from standing around the area too long. I wonder how long it would take to kill you?" General Bast tells his guest.

The faces of the Generals guest are looking very worried, hoping they do not have to remain in the area.

"Private, escort our guest back to the truck," General says. Once away, Major Star inquires. "Sir, I don't remember the dead animals were here yesterday."

"That's because they were not here yesterday. I had them laid out to add a little fear." General Bast explained.

chapter fifteen

Final exam

The following two weeks, black smoke of diesel fuel billowed the sky. Around the clock, the dump site burned, then the soil was tilled, then burned again and again. Now tons of lime is mixed with the ground then removed to a safe location.

On his trip back to the camp, Major Star stops by Gahou's home to see if she has any issues.

"Even though the waste site is getting cleaned up, many people are still ill.

We will seal some of the wells and others treated with chemicals to purify the water until the soil naturally filters itself." Major Star tells Gahou.

" Major-san, time will heal the scars of war to a certain extent, with the hope of learning from it.

That is enough talk of the past; the future is more promising. Major-san, do you have time to spare?" Gahou asked him. "I do. What do you have on your mind?" asked the Major.

"It is time for someone to show if she is worthy of being in my house. Follow me. I will escort you to a room." Gahou informs Star.

Gahou shows the Major to a room. "Please kneel. Sakusha will be here in a few minutes. She does not know it is her time." Gahou says.

"You're asking Sakusha to perform without any notice," says Major Star. "It is what I expect of a geisha. A life of grace and discipline is what we strive for." Gahou tells the Major.

Gahou steps out of the room, and the Major waits for Sakusha's arrival.

An American who is not a custom to sitting in a seiza position could be painful if prolonged.

It's been five minutes; now, the Major begins to squirm as he starts to lose the feeling in his legs.

Gahou enters the room, placing a small table in front of the Major; Sakusha enters soon after carrying a basket.

Kneeling across the Major, Sakusha carefully empties the basket, laying them out on the table.

Half of the table is a small vase and assorted plants; the other half of the table Shakusha sets up for the tea ceremony, and the little teapot with heated water.

Starting with the ikebana arrangement; Piece by piece, Sakusha arranges the plants in the vase as she explains the meaning; when she finished, Sakusha waits for Gahou's reaction. Standing behind the Major, Gahou smiles.

The next ceremony is crucial for Sakusha to continue with her training. She had to perform the ceremony correctly; she has to instruct the Major what to do with grace and tradition.

Gahou congratulates Sakusha for performing the two tasks satisfactorily. "Thank you for giving us your time Major-san," says Gahou.

Simultaneously, Major Star and Sakusha fall to their side are as they try to stand. Major Star is due to his leg's lack of circulation; for Sakusha, it is a more serious reason.

"Miss Chitosa!" Star shouts as he tries to get the feeling back into his legs. "Gahou-san, what's wrong with Chitosa-san?" Major Star asked as he recovered the use of his legs. "Major-san, Sakusha has a fever," states Gahou.

Placing his hand upon Sakusha's forehead, the Major confirms Gahou's suspicions.

"You're right, Gahou-san. Help me get Chitosa to the jeep; she needs a doctor," says Star. "Will you take her to the medical site you set up in town?" Gahou asked. "I would, but they have no more beds available. I'll take her to the camp. Could you ride with us to the camp? I need someone to hold her." Major Star asked Gahou. "Yes, I will go with you," she replies.

"Hold on tight to her; it's going to get bumpy."

The Major speeds to the camp, ignoring the rough roads, poor Gahou, she's doing what she can hold on to Sakusha and not bouncing out of the jeep.

The sentry at the gate salutes as the Major Star's jeep speeds through the entrance.

Major Star enters the medical ward with Sakusha in his arms.

"Doctor, do you have room for one more? The medical tent in town is full."

"Put her over there." Captian Sear points to an open cot.

" She fainted, plus she has a fever. Does she have cholera?" Major Star asked.

"Let's take a look at her. Uhm, she doesn't have cholera; she does have a fever. I think she has an infection that's the cause of the illness.

Get her to take this pill, with rest her fever should break." Captian Sear tells the Major.

"What kind of pill is this?" Star asked. "It's the latest miracle drug. It's called penicillin." "How do I get her to take it? She's unconscious?" the Major asked.

"You can crush the pill and give it to her with water." suggested the captain. "She still unconscious. How does that help me?" Major Star asked. "You'll find a way." says the captain with a smirk on his face.

Mixing the crushed pill in a glass of water, Star tries lifting Sakusha's head to get her to take the medication, only to have it run off her lips. Star remembers Sear's expression when he spoke about finding a way.

Gahou is startled when Major Star, then takes a mouthful of medication lifts Sakusha's head, placing his lips to hers.

After giving Sakusha her medication, Major Star turns his attention to Gahou.

"You have a choice; I take you back home or stay here overnight and wait for Miss Chitosa to wake?" "Where will I stay?" asked Gahou. "I'm sure Okina will not mind having company for the night."

chapter sixteen

Blossom

 Residents of Kyoto begin to get their lives back to normal as the cholera outbreak is under control. Even with penicillin, many elderly locals have died.

 Major Star receives a dispatch from General Bast, ordering him to report to Tokyo.

 "Sir, Do you have an idea what the General wants with you?" Sergeant Kazinski asked. "I don't know. He's probably not pleased with me due to all the headaches I've caused him. I'll find out when I see him." Major Star tells Sergeant Kazinski.

 General Bast sits at his desk dealing with various matters of managing his command when there's a knock on his door. "Come in." says the General.

"Major Star enters the room. Standing at the attention, he salutes. "Major Star reporting as commanded, Sir."

"At ease Major. I didn't call you here to chew your ass. Have a seat." Bast tells Star.

"May I ask why you asked me to come here, Sir?" "You will know soon enough.

I've seen your record, and I know why you're still at your rank. Since you took command of the Kyoto district, I have received several letters and calls about how you have handled all the adversity.

Major Star, please stand up."

General Bast walks up to the Major. "By order of the Army of the United States of American, you are promoted to Lieutenant Colonel. Congratulations, Lieutenant Colonel Star."

Colonel Star salutes. "Thank you, Sir!" "You earned it, Colonel; now return to your district; keep up the good work" General Bast tells Star.

Exiting the General's building, Sergeant Kazinski eagerly waits to know the outcome of his commander's meeting.

"Major, what did they say?" Kazinski asked. " If you look closely, it's not Major, First Sergeant. You will address me as Colonel from now on." "Colonel? Major, the General, called you here for the promotion. Congratulation Sir.

"Wait, you just called me First Sergeant," states Kazinski. "That's correct. I expect you to have the correct chevrons on your sleeve when we return to the camp. Let's not screw around here any longer; I have someplace I need to be." Colonel Star tells Kazinski.

The reason for Colonel Star's rush is, today he's taking Sakusha on a picnic.

At the geisha's house, Sakusha is trying to explain to the other women that she is not going to Kyoto or going shopping in any way.

"Gahou-san, you tell these greedy women that I will not be shopping on my personal day. I have other plans with Major-san. " Sakusha says.

"If you are not going shopping with the Major; Where are you going?" Gahou asked. "If you must know, he is taking me on a picnic," Sakusha tells Gahou.
"Oh! A picnic, you say. Where to?" Gahou asked. "I know a location that still has the cherry blossoms in bloom." Sakusha says. "I wish you well. Still, I was hoping you would go shopping." "You too! Please give me your list and the others as well. I cannot promise them anything. It will be up to Major Star-san if he wishes to look for these items." Sakusha insisted.

"Colonel, do you have everything you need?" Sergeant Kazinski asked. "I think so; sandwiches, tea, wine, everything's here." So what's in the box?" Kazinski asked. "It's a little trinket I picked up in Tokyo. A thank you gift for

Miss Chitosa. I feel guilty for her getting ill. I asked a lot from her during the plague; then she had to study hard to prepare for her exam using me as a subject." Colonel Star tells Kazinski.

"I'm sure whatever it is, she will like it, Sir. Have a good day." First Sergeant Kazinski says, saluting.

Colonel Star is at the front door of Gahou's house. He gently knocks on the wood frame of the silkscreen door. Gahou slides the door open, greeting the Colonel with a smile.

"Please come in, Major Star-san." Gahou says, not noticing the change in Star's rank. Star is not concerned if Gahou continues to call him Major. Instead, he has gotten accustomed to being called Major-san. Another day he'll bring up the change in rank.

"Major Star-san, if you wait here, Sakusha will be here in a minute," Gahou informs him.

Star's mind is focused on the silkscreen door as he waits for Sakusha. He turns when he hears Sakusha's voice.

"I hope I have not kept you waiting too long." Star turns around, finding his senses overwhelmed.

Standing before him is Sakusha dressed in a beautiful pink kimono ordained with a snowflake pattern outlined with a broad red ribbon. Her obi is bright blue, red, and pink. The sight of her nearly brought tears to his eyes.

"I have to say; You look stunning in your kimono," Star says. "Thank you. This outfit is a little bit of everyone here. Many of the women contributed something to what I am wearing." Sakusha says. "You will have to thank them for their great taste.

Do you know where we are going?" Star asked Sakusha. "I do. Since it's spring, there is a location where the war did not damage. I will give you the directions."

Sakusha stares at Star for a moment, noticing his rank insignia is different. "The leaf on your hat is a different color. has your rank changed?" Sakusha asked him.

"It's nice that you noticed; I can't say as much for my sergeant noticing the promotion to Light Colonel. We will discuss my promotion later if you wish. We should find this place you want to go." says Star.

Sakusha's directions take the Colonel to a grove of cherry trees in full bloom with a pond and small temple nestled in the center.

"Wow! I never thought a place so picturesque existed. How do you know about this place?" Star asked. "I visited here with my parents when I was a child. My sister and I loved this place." Sakusha says.

"A sister? I thought you were an only child." Colonel Star inquired. "I have an older sister who my parents have shamed. I was not allowed to mention her name." "Chitosa-san, it's sad to be forced not to acknowledge your blood. I hope she's doing well."

"I do not know. I have not seen my sister in years. Let's not talk about her; I wish to talk about you. Will your life change with your promotion?" Sakusha asked.

"Not really. My promotion is what it should be for the people I command. My past delayed what my rank should be." Colonel Star explained.

Star and Sakusha lay out a blanket beneath the cherry blossom trees. "Chitosa-san, I have to apologize for the selection of food. My cook does not know Japanese cuisine. I have small sandwiches, cookies, strawberries, and tea." Colonel Star explains.

  "What you have is fine. I have not had strawberries in years; I am partial to pastries." Sakusha tells Star.

  "I did buy you this to thank you for your help when the cholera outbreak started."

  Opening the box, Sakusha's eyes open with surprise; wrapped in a cloth is a beautiful hand-made ornate comb.

  "Star-san, where did you get this?" Sakusha asked. "Bought at a small stand in Tokyo. Its beauty caught my attention." Colonel Star says. "Colonel Star-san, this is someone's family heirloom. The person who sold it to you must have been desperate for money." Sakusha explained.

  "It was an elderly couple who sold it. The price they were asking was so under priced; I paid them three times what they were asking. The elderly woman seemed relieved when I said it was a gift for someone special."

Tears well up in Sakusha's eyes. "Star-san, please kiss me. I want to be awake when your lips touch mine." Sakusha pleads.

chapter seventeen

Understanding

Star leans towards Sakusha, gently caressing her face; he kisses her. Sitting upright, Colonel Star says. "Is that what you wanted?" "Yes. Thank you."Sakusha replies. "You are welcome," says Star.

"Thank you for the comb. I will cherish it," says Sakusha holding close to her heart. "Chitosa-san, before this goes any farther, I don't think either of us is ready to change our way of life. Am I correct assuming you want to remain a geisha?" Sakusha nods, confirming the Colonel is correct.

It is the same for me. I do find you very beautiful and innocent. I also enjoy your company. I think it's best we keep our meetings to once a month on your day off if that is fine with you." Colonel Star suggested.

Sakusha nods in agreement. "This is all your fault," Sakusha tells the Colonel. "Why is being attracted to me my fault?" Star asked. "Three times you saved my life, twice you kissed me. How am I to fight against being attracted to you." Sakusha tells Star.

"Let's get your facts correct. I saved you four times and kissed you once. Force-feeding your medicine does not count as a kiss.

Falling building, yakuza, and getting sick; you should be more careful. I may not be there to save you next time. I would be distraught with grief if were to die." Colonel Star tells Sakusha.

Sakusha lowers her head. "I am sorry for causing you so many problems. It was not my intention to do so." "It's o.k. If I had not found you in the rubble, to begin with, I would not have done so much helping your people through these trying times. I think it's wise to take one day at a time. In our case, one month at a time.

 Right now, I want to enjoy the beauty that's in front of me."

 "Colonel Star -san, I am ashamed to ask a favor from you," Sakusha says. "First, call me Frank. What is the favor?" Star asked. Sakusha hands Star a piece of paper. "They were relentless. I told them I cannot promise to get what is on the list." "Let's see. It's all in Japanese; I will have Captain Soyu translate when I return to the base. I'll see what I can do." Colonel Star says.

 "Could you also please call me Sakusha instead of Chitosa." " Sakusha is a pretty name; I look forward to saying it more often," says Star.

 Sakusha and Frank spend the rest of the day enjoying each other's company.

Returning to their duties, Colonel Star with his men and Sakusha continuing her training.

It finally happened; Sakusha had her first client as a geisha. She will have Gahou accompanying her, not only to see how she fairs but for her safety as well.

"Chitosa-san, you know what I expect from you; What I need to know, will there be a problem with Major Star-san? I know you have become very close to him." Gahou tells Sakusha.

"It is Colonel Star-san. Frank understands our situations. There will not be any problems performing my duties." Sakusha assured Gahou.

Colonel Star calls for his servant Okina to come to his office. "You asked for me, Colonel Star-san," says Okina. "Yes. Normally I would ask Captian Soyu to translate this letter from the geishas. In this case, there may be some personal items the women requested. Better for you, less embarrassing for him." says the Colonel.

Okina starts reading the list; "You are correct about more personal items. It seems the geisha have heard of a product that will aid them when it is that time of the month. It looks like that's the only thing there is on the list." says Okina.

"I get it. I'll contact a friend in Tokyo. I'll see if he can find some." says Star. "If you find some Colonel Star-san, I could use some as well," suggested Okina. "I will keep that in mind," Star says.

"Colonel-san, if you do not mind me asking; How is it going with Chitosa?" Okina asked. "You are a nosey servant," says Star. "If you do not wish to say, it is your choice," states Okina. "I don't mind talking about her. We're taking one step at a time. We agreed not to interfere in each other's business. She is a geisha

and will not deprive her of that life."
Star tells Okina. "The big question is,
how long. Relations can go two ways;
they fade or grow. If the latter happens,
what will you do?" Okina says to Colonel
Star.

"We will deal with that if or when it
happens. Are you done interrogating
me?" Star says. "For now," Okina tells
Star.

A week goes by when an unexpected
guess stands at the front gate in tears.

chapter eighteen

Heart's sake

Sakusha Chitosa stands at the entrance of the Army camp, pleading to speak to Colonel Star.

Over his radio, Colonel Star receives a message from the sentry. "Colonel Star, there is a Japanese woman who is very upset insisting on speaking to you." The guard informed Colonel; Star. "Who is she?" Star asked. "Her name is Sakusha Chitosa." replies the soldier. " Keep her at the gate. I will send Okina to escort her to my office." Star tells the sentry. "As you say, sir."

"Miss Chitosa, someone will be here in a minute to escort you to Colonel Star."

"Chitosa-san, why are you here with those eyes?" Okina asked her. "I need to speak to Star-san. It is important!" insisted Shakusha. "If it is that important, follow me; I will take you to him," Okina instructs Sakusha.

Tear-stained and bloodshot, Sakusha steps into Star's office. "What is so terrible that you walked to the camp?" Star asked Sakusha.

"It's personal," replies Sakusha. "Okina, do you mind stepping out for a minute?" Colonel Star asked her. "You do not have to ask; I do work for you. If you need me, you where to find me," states Okina.

"O.k. now we are alone; what has you in this state of mind?" Star asked. "Last night, I had my first client. The man requested me by name. Since it was my first request, Gahou accompanied me.

Everything went well. I did not notice that the client slipped this paper into my clothing. As I read the letter, I realized it was from my sister Kaori." Sakusha tells Star.

"What did the letter say?" Start asked. "She wants me to help her come home," Sakusha explained. "Where is she?" Colonel Star got an ominous feeling when he asked. "Where is your sister?"

"She is on Hokkaido. The Russian soldiers will not let anyone leave the island. The people are starving, and the women are taken advantage of."

There's a knock on Colonel Star's door. "I'm busy. Can it wait?" shouts Star. "I do not think so," Okina says as Gahou enters the room. "I wish you luck, Star-san," says Okina.

"Before you leave Okina, you can tell First Sergeant Kazinski to come in since he's laughing. You might as well stay." Colonel Star tells her.

"Colonel Star-san, I will take this impetuous child back home. I will make certain she gets a beating. Chitosa had no right to ask you for help. I stopped her when she tried to leave last night." Gahou says.

"Leave me alone; I will do as I choose!" Sakusha shouts.

Gahou and Sakusha begin to struggle as Gahou attempts to pull her out of the room.

Colonel Star's patients begin to wear thin as he listens to the women fight and shout at each other.

Having Okina and Kazinski trying to hold back their laughter does not help. After ten minutes of squabbling, Colonel Star has had enough. As loud as he can, the Colonel shouts. "That's enough!! Stand at attention!!" The room fell in silence.

First Sergeant Kazinski and Okina knew not to speak when Colonel used that tone of voice, but Gahou and Sakusha began to quarrel again. "If either of you says another word, I will slap the both of you in the guardhouse!"

Star directs to Gahou and Sakusha. The threat of being locked up got their undivided attention.

"Sakusha, Gahou sit!" Star commands. "This sister of yours, how did this person get in and out of Hokkaido?" Colonel Star asked Sakusha. "He enters by boat at night; he deals in the black market. My sister gave him the letter." Sakusha explains. "I wonder what she had to give him as payment," Star says to himself.

"Sir, you're not thinking of going to Hokkaido. If either side discovers you, your career or life will be over." Sergeant Kazinski says.

"Listen to your First Sergeant, Colonel-san; going to Hokkaido is too dangerous. I have heard stories of how the Russians treat those who try to enter or leave their domain." Gahou warns Star.

"Everyone, calm down! I haven't decided to do anything yet. Sakusha let

Okina look at your letter." Colonel Star asked her.

Since Okina has been working for Star, the Colonel notices that she is very quick at pointing out small details that most would not think twice on. She may see something in the letter other than the message.

Immediately Okina picks up on a spelling mistake, then another and another.

"That is strange. Chitosa, is your sister illiterate?" Okina asked her. "No. She is an educated woman, in more way than she should be." Sakusha says.

"Colonel Star-san, I need pencil and paper, please. I believe there is a hidden message in the letter, or this woman is an idiot." Okina states.

The encryption is a simple one, Okina deciphers the message in a couple of minutes.

"Colonel Star-san, if you decide to rescue this woman, you will find her near Lake Akan at Kotan.

It seems she is hiding in an Ainu village. She intentionally misspelled characters to protect herself in case the letter fell into the wrong hands." says Okina.

Star lowers his head, rubbing his hand over his face. "You have made up your mind, from the look on your face, you are going to Hokkaido," Okina says.

Colonel Star turns to Okina. "You are way too clever to be a simple housewife with children. Who are you?" Star asked her.

"It's about time you asked about my past. I am, or I was a housewife, but I was far from straightforward; I was in the inelegance division during the war. If those egotistical bastard men had listened to me, there would have been a lot fewer meaningless deaths. I'm not saying we would have won the war. The

American economy crushed us from the start.

I tried to warn the generals that America's might could be catastrophic If we continued to fight. Those idiots learned the hard way, with the destruction of two cities."

Star smiles. "Your husband must have been very proud to love you," says Star. "The hell he was! That bastard needed his butt kicked constantly. He kept trying to make me into the perfect obedient wife. If he were still alive, I would still be kicking his butt.

We are getting off the subject; if you are going to Hokkaido, you need a plan." Okina suggested.

chapter nineteen

Preparations

"Colonel, if you're considering going to Hokkaido, I'm coming with you." First Sergeant Kazinski says. "I wouldn't want it anyway, Sergeant. A certain annoying woman will be coming with us as well. I don't know what her sister looks like." says Colonel Star.

"Colonel-san, the village Sakusha's sister is staying is not coastal. You will have to travel at least thrifty miles inland to reach it.

You are going to need me to go with you as well. I know Hokkaido. Besides, I am your servant. Your capture will lose me a good-paying job and a place to sleep.

The military was aware of the black market trade route leading into Hokkaido. However, we did not pay much attention because they had more significant problems.

Gahou-san and I will find someone who will take us across. We could take the shortest route to the island, but it means we will have to travel overland four times longer. I prefer avoiding as many checkpoints as possible." Okina suggested.

"You are more impressive every day," says Star. "Thank you. I am a widower; if you decide you are looking for experience, I am available." Okina jokes. "It's tempting, but I decline, because I would need a cushion to sit on very often.

For this trip, we'll need clothing, food, and something to use as a bribe if required." Colonel states.

    "Colonel-san, Gahou will inform you when we have secured transportation. It will take us one or two days to arrange it." Okina says.

    "It looks like we have a plan. Okina, do you mind having guest for the night? It's getting late. I'll have Sergeant Kazinski give them a ride home tomorrow.

    "I do not mind the company," says Okina. "I'll have blankets and pillows sent to your house, and dinner will be ready in the mess hall in one hour." Colonel Star tells the ladies.

    Entering the mess tent with three women, some of the other soldiers start whispering between each other. Some whisper out of curiosity and some out of resentment. First Sergeant Kazinski picks up on one conversation in particular. It is unpleasant and has a tone of violence towards Gahou.

Kazinski walks to the soldier's table, placing his head between them, with an arm around each of them.

"You can whisper all you want about these ladies, but if I hear this conversation again, there will not be a court-martial, just a deadly accident." The First Sergeant's warning does not go unnoticed by the soldiers and Gahou.

She watched the First Sergeant as he walked up to the two soldiers. She saw fear in the eyes of the two men. Whatever the Sergeant said, it had a profound effect on their complexion.

After Kazinski finished talking, he returned to the Colonel's table, sitting beside Gahou.

Staring at Kazinski, Gahou says. "What just happened between you and those men, Sergeant-san?"

Gahou has known the First Sergeant from the first day she met the Colonel. Her perception of Kazinski has been crude, slightly vulgar, rough around the edges, which fit the Sergeants complexion, scared and rough-looking from the war.

That's why Gahou was so surprised by the First Sergeant's reply to her question.

"They were having a disturbing conversation about someone I know. I kindly said, continue with that line of talk; it will be detrimental to your health." "Who was the person they were discussing?" Gahou asked. "They were talking about you." First Sergeant Kazinski replied.

Gahou is not a naive little girl. She is in her mid-thirties and had cared for many geishas while surviving the war.

She is finding it difficult to believe what just happened to her. Staring at Kazinski's war-tattered face, her heart begins to pound, causing her face to flush.

Looking away, surprised, Gahou looks at Kazinski again to confirm that she is attracted to the rough-hued face of the First Sergeant.

Kazinski's act of nobility and honor unwittingly stole Gahou's heart, and she is finding it difficult dealing with the emotion.

"Gahou, are you feeling well? You look a little red in the face." Colonel Star asked her. "I am fine. I am a little tired." Gahou says.

That evening Okina, Sakusha, and Gahou are covered with blankets, getting ready to sleep. Sakusha has noticed Gahou is more quiet than usual. "Gahou-san, are you feeling well? You have not spoken since dinner." Sakusha asked her.

"I am fine! " she shouts. "If there is a problem, maybe I can help," Sakusha suggested. "There is nothing you can do to help me. I discovered something that has me a little unsettled. You do not have to worry; it is nothing bad. I do not wish to talk about it. Get some sleep;

we are going to have a busy day tomorrow." Gahou tells Sakusha.

It takes a little more than two days for Okina and Gahou to secure passage to Hokkaido; almost two weeks go by before they find someone to ferry them secretly to the island.

They meet one more time before leaving for Hokkaido, Colonel Star and Okina go over the plan, ensuring all is ready.

"Colonel-san, the boatman will take us outside of Shiranoka; from there, we will have to improvise the rest of the way. We should get to Kota in two days. The boatman will return to pick us up at Shiranoka in a week. If we are late, he will not wait or return for us, so let us be on time." Okina stressed.

" I have secured traditional clothing for everyone, with plenty of military rations. If we need to bribe Russians, I did not skimp on the booze we will take along; top-quality vodka and single malt scotch. The base will not miss the Sergeant and me; Officially, we are on vacation.

I have a staff car at my disposal to take us to the coast. I'm sure we can find someplace to hide the car while we are away. Okina, I want you and Sakusha to start walking to the base in the morning. The First Sergeant and I will pick you up on the way. If no one has questions, I will see you tomorrow morning." says Star.

chapter twenty

Nameless Ainu

Early morning Colonel Star discovers an extra person walking down the road with Okina and Sakusha.

"Gahou, what are you doing here?" Colonel Star asked. "I am going with you. Do not ask why; I have my reasons." Gahou tells Star. "What is in the basket?" the Colonel asked. " Trust me, in an emergency, this will come in handy," Gahou says. "Hop in. We need to get to the coast," says Sergeant Kazinski.

"Okina, I am curious; What did you offer as payment for passage to Hokkaido?" Colonel Star asked. "I hope you brought plenty of liquor. The boat owner enjoys his drink as much as the

Russians." "I have two cases of vodka and scotch. I won't mind parting with half. High-quality booze will sell for a fortune on the black market. Our captain knows that as well." Colonel Star states.

Colonel Star and his party wait for nightfall and their transportation at a secluded dock.

"Colonel, I hear a motor coming our way. Can you see anything?" Sergeant Kazinski asked. "If this captain is smart, he will keep his deck light off until he's certain no one is following him."

The boat captain flashes a light towards the shore, Gahou returns his signal.

Once the boat docks, the captain refuses to allow anyone to board until paid.

"Colonel Star, the captain, wishes to be paid," Okina informs him. "O.k. Sergeant, bring over the crate." Kazinski sets down a box filled with half vodka and scotch. To make sure he is not getting conned, the captain takes one of the bottles of scotch. Removing the cap, he takes a large swallow.

If you know your scotch, a single malt of high quality is very potent. Immediately the captain begins to cough and choke as his throat turns to fire.

Colonel Star worried for a moment because of the captain's reaction; it lasted until the captain smiled, giving a thumbs up.

Through the evening, the small boat's engine chugged along until it came with the insight of Hokkaido. The captain turns off his engine, unfurling his sail, making sure there are no lights on his boat and onshore scanning for him.

"Frank-san, how can the captain see where he is going?" Sakusha asked. "The captain has made this trip many times, he could probably do it with his eyes closed." Star says. The captain shushes Star and Sakusha as he is nears the shore.

Safely tied to shore, Star and his party exit the boat. The Colonel observes the captain's expression as Kazinski removes the liquor from the second create, putting it into rucksacks.

"First Sergeant, hand me one of those bottles of vodka," Star says. "There you go, Sir," Kazinski says. Removing the cap, Star takes a health swig then hands it to the captain. "Stay safe," Star says. The captain smiles, then take a gulp of vodka." "I will," he replied.

The captain does not remain long as soon as everyone in onshore he leaves.

"Okina, it will dawn soon; you said you're familiar with Hokkaido. Which way do we go? " Colonel Star asked. "We go northeast towards Kushiro. We should come to one of the roads that go north. I hope there are not many check checkpoints along the way." Okina tells the Colonel.

At first, it was difficult traveling in the dark; as the sun started to rise, Colonel Star and his party began to cover more ground.

Resting several times for the women, they did not reach one of the roads leading from Kushiro until late afternoon.

"It will be dark and cold soon; we need to find a place to rest for the night," Okina suggested.

"It's spring; how cold can it get during the night?" Colonel Star asked Okina. "If the wind blows in the right direction, it could get below freezing," Okina tells the Colonel. "I want everyone to keep their eyes open for any kind of shelter." Colonel Star informs the others.

The farther north they walked, the deeper into the mountains with no sign of any shelter they could find.

The sun was dropping over the horizon; Colonel Star could feel the temperature dropping rapidly.

"First Sergeant, we have no choice; we have to make some type of shelter. The women will not survive a sub-freezing night." Colonel Star tells him.

"Frank-san, what is that over there in those trees?" Sakusha points.

A dome building made of straw and branches camouflaged against the background of the forest.

" Let's find out if someone is living there," Sakusha says. "What kind of building is it?" Colonel Star asked Okina. "I believe it is Ainu structure, "Okina tells him. "Walking up to the building, an elderly weather face man opens the door.

"Can we stay for the night?" Colonel Star asked the man. "I do not think he understands you, Star-san. Many Ainu do not speak Japanese, and I do not speak Ainu," says Okina.

The older man dressed in modern clothes mixed with animal skins leans to look behind Star, sees Sakusha and Gahou shivering.

He steps back into his home, the Ainu signals everyone to enter.

Inside, Star finds it warm and cozy with a small fire in the center of the house with a small opening on the ceiling.

The old Ainu speaks to Star, repeating the exact phrase over. "Okina, do you have any idea what he is asking me?" Colonel Star asked. "I think he is trying to ask where are we traveling?" "Kota," Star says to the old man. "Kota," the Ainu replies, nodding his head.

The older man speaks again to Star as he scribes a map of the area on the dirt floor. He points out where they are and the road they are on; also, he draws a line across the street ahead of where the cabin is on his map. He begins to march and speak to Star.

Realizing what he is describing, Star nods he understands. "What is he telling you?" Gahou asked. "He said there is a checkpoint a few miles up the road. We'll have to think of a way to get past it. That is why I brought the booze.

You and the other women should take a sip of the scotch; it will warm you up." Star says.

Each woman takes a sip; The old Ainu licks his lips holding out his hand. Star hands him the bottle. To his belief, he sees the old geezer suck down the bottle without taking a breath. The old guy nods his head, agreeing with the flavor of the scotch.

"Sir, I would hate to drink what that guy is used to drinking. He didn't even blink an eye drinking that bottle." Sergeant Kazinski says. "It's a big world, Sergeant." the Colonel replies.

The sun has been up a couple of hours; everyone is awake. The Colonel shares his military rations with his new friend. When ready to leave, each take turns to bow, thanking the old Ainu before continuing their journey. Colonel Star hands a bottle of vodka to the Ainu to thank him.

"Colonel, do you have a plan to get past the checkpoint?" Sergeant Kazinski asked him. "I'm working on it. I need to have a peek at how many guards there are to start." Colonel Star says with some uncertainly.

"Colonel-san, leave the guards to me," Gahou tells him. "What are you going to do?" Star asked her." I will be your distraction. What is in this basket will make it so. Tools of the trade." says Gahou.

"I know what you are going to do; I will do it." insisted Sakusha. "I think not Chitosa-san. I was an experienced geisha before I became the mother of the house. These Russians are not like our clients; they can be unpredictable and dangerous. So before we arrive at the checkpoint, I will change clothes Chitosa will apply the makeup." Gahou informs the Colonel.

The road to Kota is narrow, with mountain peaks and ravines on either side. Colonel Star does not enjoy surprises; he sends his First Sergeant on an errand.

"First Sergeant, I want you to go ahead of us. During the war, you were skilled in using the landscape to your advantage. I need you to assess the checkpoint's vulnerability. I prefer getting past it undetected." "I'm on my way, Sir." replies the First Sergeant." Do not take chances." Gahou tells Kazinski. "I will be cautious. I appreciate your concern." Kazinski replies.

The First Sergeant leaves Star and the ladies behind as he runs ahead. According to the Ainu, the checkpoint is roughly three to four miles down the road.

Colonel Star keeps the pace of walking as easy as possible. If needed, he would like the women rested enough to escape into the forest if discovered by a Russian patrol.

Sakusha is young but not blind, noticing Gahou's actions are out of character. Her concern for the First Sergeant has piqued her interest.

"Gahou-san, what is the real reason you decided to come with us? Is it because you interested in Colonel-san' s Sergeant?" Sakusha asked her.

"What are you saying? I do not have an attachment towards the First Sergeant." Gahou stated.

"There nothing wrong if you do, though his features are too raw and scared for my taste," Sakusha says with a slight grin.

"When you have matured, you will understand there is more to like in how a person looks. How that person's looks could mean less, as the relationship grow. That is enough talking about me." Gahou tells Sakusha as she walks ahead of her. Sakusha smiles from the trap results she set to get information on Gahou's state of mind or heart.

Colonel Star and the women continue walking towards the checkpoint, stopping when the First Sergeant returns with needed information.

"First Sergeant, how are our chances of getting past the Russians at the checkpoint?" Colonel Star asked. "They look fare. There is a ravine on one side of the guard post which we can cross if we do not make too much noise and the two guards are not too diligent." Sergeant Kazinski reports.

"I can help with if the guards are diligent, Sergeant Kazinski -san. How far ahead is this checkpoint?" Gahou asked. "It is around the next turn," Kazinski says.

chapter twenty-one

Reunion

"Colonel Star-san and Sergeant Kazinski -san, remain here. Sakusha, you follow me into those trees and bring the basket." Gahou instructs her.
"Hold still while I apply the face paint," Sakusha says. "Skip the face paint. Apply the eyes and lips only." Gahou says. "No face paint? Is it because you think someone may not approve of you wearing it?" suggested Sakusha. "Speak again about my personal life; you will lose your next three personal days." The threatening expression on Gahou's tells Sakusha she may have gone too far with her prodding. "Forgive me." humbly Sakusha says.

"First Sergeant, I want you to watch Gahou when she speaks with the Russians. If her situation becomes dangerous, you know what to do." Colonel Star tells him. I understand, Sir." replies Kazinski.

Gahou and Sakusha return to the group; for First Sergeant Kazinski, he's getting to look at Gahou in a new light, seeing her as she is now, softeners his hard chiseled face. "Gahou" slips from Kazinski's lips.

Gahou and the Sergeant's eyes meet for a split second. Sometimes that's all it takes to connect.

"Gahou, Sergeant Kazinski will follow you from a distance. If it looks like you are in any danger, he will act accordingly.

We will use the ravine to pass the guards. Gahou, we will depend on your beauty and charm." Colonel Star tells her. "I will do my best, Colonel-san. I

need one bottle of vodka and scotch."
Gahou tells Star.

As Gahou walks in sight of the guards, they call her forward. Neither knows each other's language except one or two words.

"What is your business?" one of the Russian soldiers asked her. Timidly, Gahou walks up to the sentries. bowing, she says, "Danna. " Gahou replies. The guards look at her strangely. "Are you geisha?" she is asked, "Gahou nods that she is. One of the guards points to the sack she is carrying.

Opening the sack, Gahou repeats it is for the client by saying the dana; the guards smile as they observe Gahou. Countering the guard's vestures towards her, she grasps the bottles tightly, displaying they cannot have the liquor.

Gahou's superior performance does what it's intended to do; the guards turn their attention to the liquor as the guard pulls the sack away from Gahou's grasp.

The guards begin drinking the liquor with a satisfying reaction; one guard signals Gahou to move along.

Gahou walks through the checkpoint and continues to walk until she is out of sight of the checkpoint not long after First Sergeant Kazinski steps onto the road.

"Gahou, are you fine? I was worried when the guards started to pay more attention to you than needed." "I am fine. I appreciate your concern." Gahou says. She walks up to Kazinski, taking his face in her hands, to kiss him.

Kazinski stares at Gahou, surprised, not because she kissed him; because she took the initiative before him. Gahou waits for the First Sergeant's reply to her kiss. It takes Kazinski a few seconds to come to his senses before taking Gahou into his arms returning the kiss.

Still in each other's arms, Kazinski says, "When?" "The day in the mess tent. When did you?" Gahou asked. "I don't know. I'm still not certain when; What do you see in me? This face I have is not the prettiest. There are a few scars from the war that will never go away." Sergeant Kazinski says.

"You may have scars on the outside; the flawlessness of your heart blinds me from seeing them," Gahou says.

"Oh! What do we have here?" says Okina. Gahou and the First Sergeant separate. "Nothing!!" Gahou and Kazinski shout.

"Okina, let them be. First Sergeant, we are not home yet; keep your mind clear. That goes for you as well, Gahou. "Colonel Star tells them. "Yes, Colonel." Gahou bows, "I will, Star-san."

"It's still a couple of miles to the Ainu town. The quicker we get there and get back to the mainland, the happier I will be," states Colonel Star.

The following two miles are uneventful for Colonel Star's party when they come upon the outskirts of Kota. The local Ainu notices the Colonel walking towards the entrance of the village. One of the villagers runs to inform the village chief.

The chief and a welcome sight greet Colonel Star. Sakusha's sister Kaori is with the village chief.

"Sakusha rushes to her sister. They embrace each other in tears. "You came!" Kaori says. "I am your sister, and I had to save you," Sakusha says.

"Who are these people?" Kaori asked. "These are the people who made being here possible. Frank Star, Gahou, Okina, and Sergeant Kazinski. " "Are they Americans?" Kaori asked. "The men are, Gahou is my house mother, Okina is Colonel Star's servant," Sakusha explains.

" This is Aterui; he is the village chief." Kaori introduces Colonel Star.

The Colonel bows. "It is a pleasure to meet you. Thank you for keeping Sakusha's sister safe." the Colonel says in Japanese.

Atarui replies in rough English. "It is a pleasure to meet you." "You speak my language?" says Star. "I learned from monks when I was a child. Follow me; you must be tired from your journey. How long will you stay?" Atarui asked Star. "Long enough for the women to rest before the journey back to the shore." Colonel Star tells the chief.

"How did you get past the Russians?" Atarui asked. "Gahou's skill and American liquor as a distraction," Star says. "You will find it more difficult getting past the Russians on your return trip. If you have more liquor, I can help you get past the checkpoint." Atarui says. Star opens his pack, displaying several bottles of vodka and scotch.

Atarui smiles at the sight of the Colonel's sack. That evening Star and

Kazinski were no match for Aterui drinking.

The following day, the women were joyful at the Colonel Star and his Sergeant's expense. "That will teach you to compete drinking with someone you do not know," Sakusha tells Star. "We had to show respect, and the chief invited us to have a few drinks with him. I think he's related to that old guy we met yesterday." Star says.

Atarui hands Gahou two bottles of liquor. "These are special bottles. Colonel Star and I came up with a plan. It would help if you chewed this root before you start drinking, or you will be sound asleep with the Russians" Atarui tells Gahou.

chapter twenty-two

Home

Colonel Star's group starts walking back to the Russian checkpoint, leading the group is Gahou. Before they get too near the checkpoint, Gahou begins to chew on the root Aterui gave her.
"This tastes terrible!" exclaimed Gahou. "You had better chew it; you might start to get heavy after carrying you a few miles." First Sergeant Kazinski says. "Are you implying that I am overweight?" replies Gahou.
"I said nothing about being fat. Your body is perfect. There is only one way to carry a dead weight body; slinging you over my shoulder." Kazinski says. "You will not carry me like a sack of grain,"

states Gahou. "Keep chewing then," says Kazinski.

"Were coming to the checkpoint, you know what to do, Gahou. We will be in the ravine while the First Sergeant watches you from a distance." Colonel Star tells her.

"Sakusha, I need you to apply a little makeup, then I will smear it. I don't want to look too good. I need the Russians to think my dana was not satisfied with me for withholding liquor." Gahou suggested. I will go ahead now, wish me luck." says Gahou.

Approaching the checkpoint, the guard commands Gahou to come forward. "It is you again. You have returned soon. From your complexion, I can tell someone was not satisfied. You are hiding something?" the guard asked her.

Gahou plays her part; she tries to keep the bottle of vodka hidden. Grabbing

Gahou's arm, the guard pulls the bottle away from her.

"Since you tried to keep it from us as well, we will retain you for questioning, not before we have a taste of this vodka.

This bottle is open. You taste first. I would not want anything wrong to happen to us first." says the guard.

Gahou opens the bottle she takes a drink. The guard says, "keep drinking." Gahou starts to guzzle the vodka. "That is enough! Give me that bottle." says the guard.

The two Russian guards proceed to drink the vodka. The extra ingredient in the vodka Gahou is immune from its effect, but not the large amount of alcohol she consumed.

The guards are feeling the effect of the drug. "What did you do to us?" says the guard grasping Gahou's arm. Gahou struggled against the guard's hold for a moment. The guard feels a sudden pain on the back of his head before falling to the ground.

"You looked like you needed some help." Sergeant Kazinski says. Gahou stares at the Sergeant's face then staggers.

"Walking straight looks to be difficult at the moment. It won't be over my shoulder; princess style should do." Kazinski says. "What are you doing? Put me down!" Gahou insisted.

"I don't know how long these idiots are going to be unconscious, and you are having trouble standing from the booze. I will let you walk after we put some distance from this place." says the First Sergeant.

Gahou holds on firmly as Kazinski walks away from the checkpoint quickly. A half-mile down the road, he meets up with the rest of the party. "How are you feeling, Gahou?' Colonel Star asked her. "Much better. I had no choice, drinking almost half a bottle of vodka. The guards were suspicious from my return." Gahou explains.

"Sir, we should move quickly towards the coast. I had to knock one of the guards out." First Sergeant Kazinski informs his commander.

"That's a useful piece of information. When those guards wake, they will sound the alarm. Ladies, it may get a little rough walking to the coast; don't be bashful if you take turns riding piggyback." Colonel Star says. "Do not worry about us Colonel -san, we will make the coast without any difficulty. We are tougher than you think." Okina says.

What had taken two days to reach Kota, Colonel Star's party walked throughout the night along roads and forest to get the location for their transportation in 24 hours.

"We made it back in time, let's hope the captain does not forget about us, or it will be a long walk and swim to the mainland.

Sakusha, how are you holding up?" Colonel Star asked her. "I am fine. A little tired and hungry," replied Sakusha. "We have time to rest before our transportation arrives. I want everyone to eat something. Military rations are not the tastiest of meals, but they will give you energy." Colonel Star says.

Darkness falls, Star waits and hopes for the small boat to arrive at his location. In the distance, Colonel Star sees a dim light signal selective flashes towards the shore, and Star responds with the proper reply.

The boat captain guides his boat to shore, where the Colonel and his party board the ship.

"You are a welcome sight. I have more liquor for you for the trip back." Colonel Star says to the captain. He bows, thanking the Colonel.

The voyage to the main island is uneventful. Exhausted from their ordeal, the women sleep in the boat's bow.

chapter twenty-three

Reconcile

"Sakusha, it's time to wake up; we're approaching the mainland." Colonel Star says, gently shaking her. "Oh? Are we? Can you lend me your hand so that I can stand?" Sakusha asked.

Star holds his hand for Sakusha to grasp. Helping her up as the boat rocks, causing the Colonel to fall forward on top of Sakusha.

Star braced himself with his hands not to have his weight on her with both of their faces are a few inches away, gazing into the eyes of each other.

"Are you hurt?" Star asked. "I am fine. Never better," replies Sakusha with a smile.

Holding his weight with one hand, Star caresses her face to kiss her.

His kiss is gentle and soft causing Sakusha's face to glow with joy.

"I should stand. How wonderful this moment is; if the others see us like this, there will be rumors." Colonel Star says. "I believe you are correct," replies Sakusha.

With a helping hand, Sakusha stands and goes out on the deck with Star. "What is your sister's plan when she returns to Kyoto?" Star asked Sakusha. "Frank-san, do not think ill of me when I say I love Kaori, but I also have a deep resentment towards her.

I do not feel good about myself with this resentment and having you put yourself in danger on my behalf. It feels like I was deceiving you." Sakusha tells Star.

Taking Sakusha in his arms, Star says, "There was no deception; you and I chose to take this journey because of love. Mine for you and yours for your sister. You and Kaori need to discuss what is troubling you; do not lessen why we rescued her. No family is perfect. Please spend some time discussing what troubles you with her. Whatever the cause for your pain might be just as painful for her. Talk to her. Leaving the problem unresolved can cause more unneeded suffering for both of you."

Unknowing Sakusha, Kaori was listening to her conversation. "I did not realize I had hurt you, Sakusha," Kaori says to her sister.

"Kaori!" surprised Sakusha says. "I'll let the two you speak to each other alone," says Star.

"If I have offended you, Sakusha, please forgive me." "Why did you leave me? You could have taken me with you." Sakusha asked. "I could not. The life I chose to follow was not an honorable one. There were times when I was in danger of my life. Mother did you a favor sending you away to be a geisha. If she had not, you would be living on the streets or dead. Mother loved you; she did the best she could to keep you safe." You may be correct." Sakusha says. "Have you seen mother lately?" Kaori asked.

"No. Soon after Gahou agreed to take me in, she disappeared. I suspect she is someplace starting a new life." Sakusha says.

"Your life did not turn out so bad. You are young and beautiful. Your face does not have the scars of hardship as mine does.

From what I can see, the American soldier and you have grown close. To do what he did to rescue me shows he is very much in love with you, and I suspect it is the same for you. There may come a time when you or he will have to choose how you wish to live your lives."

Tears begin to well up in Sakusha's eyes. Kaori, the older and wiser sister, takes Sakusha in her arms.

The captain docks his boat. Before Colonel Star steps off, he gives the captain the last bottles of liquor left, making him very grateful.

The staff car is still where Star hid it. The first stop made is Gahou's home, where Sakusha. Kaori and Gahou prepare the wash the sweat and dirt of their journey from them. Colonel Star and Sakusha stare into each other's eyes, wanting to kiss, each holding back because of their circumstances.

Arriving at the base, Okina looks at the man in tattered Japanese army clothing standing outside the base gate, she shouts, "Stop the car!" Stepping from the car she rushes to the man.

"Hondo, is that you?" says Okina. "Yes, it is my wife. I finally found you." Hondo tells his wife.

Okina wraps her arms around her husband. "I thought you were dead. I got a letter from the war office saying so." "It was a mistake, another soldier had my name tag, I was in a coma, so no one knew who I was."

"How did you find me?" Okina asked. "When I arrived where our home used to be, I noticed the small shrine where our children are. In the shrine was a message explaining where to find you." Hondo explained.

Okina turns to look at the Colonel with a thankful smile.

"Colonel, who is that person?" Sergeant Kazinski asked. "I believe it's her husband who she thought was dead." Colonel Star replied.

The subsequent events between Okina and her husband caught the Colonel and Kazinski by surprise, they were no longer the loving couple.

Okina is having a heated argument with her husband. Hondo makes the mistake of grabbing his wife's arm, she places her knee between his legs sending him to the ground gasping for air.

Okina is speaking to her husband loud enough, Colonel can hear her. "I am not your slave. You cannot boss around like the other women! You and I are equal, or you will be in more pain. Do you understand?" Okina points out to her husband.

Star walks up to Hondo. "Is everything alright?" "Damn liberated woman," Hondo replies.

"Do not blame me for her attitude," Star says. "You had nothing to do with her obstinate one reason why I love her. Sometimes I think dying in battle might have been the better option," says Hondo. Kneeling beside her husband, Okina says, "Do not ever say that! I love you! I was devastated when I received notice of your death.

"Hondo-san, when you catch your breath, I'll give you a ride to where your wife is living. I'm sure the two of you have a lot to say. Besides, your wife is starting to scare the sentry at the gate." Colonel Star says.

chapter twenty-four

Crossroad

"Sir, do you think anyone knows where we went?" First Sergeant Kazinski asked. "If anyone does, you and I will be looking for new jobs. I hope you're not regretting coming along.

Look on the bright side; you and I will have a place to live if discovered. I'm sure Sakusha and Gahou will enjoy our company." says the Colonel.

There's a knock on the Colonel's door. "Yes," replies Star. "It is I, Okina, and my husband, Star-san. May we come in?" she asked. "Please come do," says Star.

"Colonel Star-san, Hondo wishes to speak to you. He has come to an understanding." Okina explains.

Hondo bows as he speaks. "Colonel Star-san, I wish to convey an apology for my actions earlier and thank you for what you have done for my wife and children. My wife has made it clear that I owe you my gratitude."

"Hondo Sakato, now that you and your wife have settled your differences, what is next on your agenda?" Colonel Star asked him.

"We still own the land where our home was. I was hoping I could stay with my wife until I could rebuild it. I will find work to purchase the materials needed." Hondo requested.

"You can stay with your wife while I employ her. Work will be difficult to come by in these times. I could put in a word to someone I know who may find work for you. I'll have Gahou reach out to a certain organization." Colonel Star tells Hondo.

" We have a head start on money. I have been saving my earnings. " Okina tells her husband. "How much money do you have?" Hondo asked his wife. "Almost two hundred American dollars," replies Okina. "Almost two hundred! What have you been doing for work?" Hondo excited asked his wife.

"Do not even think what you are thinking, or it will be painful. You have been missing for almost two years. In that time, I have been working for the Colonel. He pays me well for the work I do. You have no idea what is required to keep that untidy person's quarters clean."

Hondo stares at Star. "It's true. I'm a slob." Colonel Star states. "I feel bad for a certain young geisha. I have not informed her what she is in for if she decides to spend her life with you." Okina tells Star.

The following year passes without any more incidents with the geisha. Hondo and Okina have started to rebuild their home; First Sergeant Kazinski is spending time together when they have the time.

Colonel Star and Sakusha's relationship has grown, making it more upsetting for both of them because rules and regulations restrict their love.

On Sakusha's next personal day, Colonel Star walks with her with something weighing heavy on his mind.

Sakusha has known Star long enough to see something is bothering him.

"Frank-san, speak to me. I see you are stressed." Sakusha says. "Sakusha, I do not wish to do this anymore," says Star. "Uh? Do you wish to leave me?" Sakusha asked. "No. I wish to marry you. To do that, I will hand in my resignation." "You cannot do that! The Army is your life." Sakusha tells Star. "The Army is not my life; you are.

I love you. I do not want to pressure you to do anything. You're a geisha; like the Army, it's a commitment. I need to think and talk to Gahou about what I am asking and how you feel. Take your time. Do not worry whether you choose to marry me or not; I will never stop loving you."

Sakusha looks at Star as tears run from her eyes. "Did I upset you?" Star says. "No. I am pleased you asked me to be your wife. I am also happy you do not require an answer at this moment. I love you. It is as you say, I should think about before making a decision." Sakusha says.

"Shall we continue our walk?" Star says. "I would love to," replies Sakusha.

That evening Sakusha discusses Frank's proposal with Gahou.

"Frank-san asked me to be his wife." "I thought he was not allowed to get involved with Japanese people," Gahou asked.

"Frank-san will resign his omission so he could marry me." Sakusha tells Gahou.

"If the Colonel is willing to go that far to be with you, do you doubt his love for you, and do you love the Colonel?" Gahou says. "I do, but I am geisha," Sakusha replies.

A warm smile glows on Gahou's face. "Over the years, a geisha's role has evolved, from prostitution to entertainers, companions.; who's say we cannot be wive' s.

You are no longer miako. I have watched you mature into a beautiful woman. It is for you to choose what path you wish to take. Married or not, you will always be geisha." Gahou explains to Sakusha.

Bowing, Sakusha thanks Gahou for her advice. "I know what I must do; thank you for the wonderful life you gave me. I will always think of you as my mother." Gahou takes Sakusha in her arms. "You will always be welcome in my family.

When will you see the Colonel again?" Gahou asked, "As soon as it takes to walk to him." says Sakusha. "If you are walking to the army camp, I will go with you for safety and to speak to the First Sergeant." Gahou states.

chapter twenty-five

Commitment

Having seen Sakusha and Gahou visit the camp many times over the last two years, the sentry at the front gate waves as pass through the front gate. "Shall I tell the Colonel you are here?" asked the guard. "I prefer you do not. I would like to surprise my husband." Sakusha replies.

It takes the sentry a few minutes to realize what Sakusha said. "Married?" the guard says to himself.

Okina and Sergeant Kazinski see Sakusha and Gahou walking towards Colonel Star's office.

"Gahou, what are you doing here?" Kazinski asked her. Gahou grasps Kazinski's hand. You stay with me,

Okina you as well. Sakusha has to discuss something important to Star-san. Both of their lives are about to change for the better." Gahou explains. "She isn't going to kill him?" states the First Sergeant. "Do not be silly. You will find out soon enough." Gahou tells Kazinski.

Sakusha knocks on the Colonel's door. "May I come in?" she asked. "Sakusha! How did you get here?" Star asked. "Gahou and I walked. Please listen to what I have to say." Sakusha kneels, sitting back on her heels. "Yes, I will marry you," she says.

Colonel Star kneels, facing her. "Is this what you want?" he asked. "It is. I spoke to Gahou about how I feel. I love you. In my heart, there is room for a life with you and geisha because I believe one has prepared me for the other." Sakusha tells Frank.

Taking Sakusha's hands into his, Colonel Star says. "If this is what you want, are you up to take a trip to Tokyo? I have to deliver my resignation in person." Sakusha smiles as tears of joy run from her eyes.

Wiping away her tears, they embrace each other while on their knees. "Sakusha, I need to ask you for a favor," Star says. "Anything, please ask," replies Sakusha. "Could you help me stand up? My knees are not as flexible as yours." "Sakusha laughs. Standing, she holds out her hand to Star.

Frank and Sakusha step outside. "First Sergeant Kazinski!" shouts Star. Rushing to his commander, the First Sergeant says. "Yes, Sir!" "First Sergeant, get me a staff car. Sakusha and I will be driving to Tokyo. We may be gone overnight. I want you to make certain Gahou finds her way home safely. She can use my quarters to stay the night if needed." Colonel Star commanded. "As you say, Sir!" the First Sergeant barked out.

Sitting beside her future husband, Sakusha feels her heart pound with anticipation. Sakusha's warm body against his as he drives to Tokyo feels like taking a trip into the country side.

"It looks like everything is coming full circle. Soon Okina will leave with her husband to live in their new home. Sergeant Kazinski and Gahou may be next on the marriage list.

We will be husband and wife. I'm confident I will find work in Japan. So how's your sister doing? Is she still struggling to support herself the honorable way?" "She is fine. Finding employment, it is a struggle; too many people remember her past life." Sakusha says. "If she continues to work hard, someone will give her a chance to prove herself," Star says.

"Frank, why do you not wish to go back to America. It is your home," says Sakusha.

"I have no family in America. I was raised in an orphanage. There is still a lot of resentment towards the Japanese. It's too early for you in America. It has been five years since the war. My home is with you in Japan. Later in the future, we will visit my home." the Colonel explained.

Sakusha snuggles closer to Star. "We are nearing Tokyo. I can see the outline of the city from here." Star says.

Standing outside General Bast's office, Frank holds Sakusha's hand as he knocks on the door.

"Come in." General Bast says. Bast immediately notices his Colonel holding hands with a Japanese woman. "What can I do for you, Colonel Star?" General Bast asked. "Sir, I am here to turn in my resignation," Star says, placing his paperwork on the General's desk.

"Could this pretty young woman be the reason for you leaving the military?" General states. "It is, Sir. I have fallen in love with this beautiful geisha. Regulation state officers are not allowed to have relations with the locals. Sakusha and I wish to get married. Leaving the Army is the only way, Sir." Colonel Star states.

Colonel Star, before considering your request, I would like to speak to this lovely young lady in private. Would that be fine with you, Miss Sakusha.?" Bast asked her.

Sakusha looks to Star, nodding, that is o.k. Star smiles. Sakusha nods she will speak to the General in private.

"Before Colonel Star steps out, may I have your full name?" General Bast asked Sakusha. "My name is Sakusha Chisato, Sir." "Miss Chisato, have a seat. It will not take long, and I will not bite you, so relax. You may go, Colonel."

chapter twenty-six

Love and war

"Miss Chisato, tell me about Colonel Star. To love him as you claim, you must know him well enough to marry. What part of him makes you the happiest?" Bast asked her.

Sakusha thinks for a moment. "This may sound strange; most people would think I would say it is his gentleness and love; for me, it is his understanding of the overall picture. He is not cruel when he needs to achieve an objective. Frank is ingenious when it comes to organizing. I love who he is.

I think it will be a significant loss when he leaves the military." says Sakusha.

"Tell me about you. You are a geisha. Will your lifestyle continue as before? A geisha must entertain clients with grace and dignity. Will that continue?" General Bast asked.

"Only with my husband. I am a young geisha, Frank-san knows as much about me as I do myself. I love him. He has done things for me that have put his life in danger." Sakusha says. "If you are talking about the trip to Hokkaido you took, I know." "You do? How?" Sakusha asked. "These stars in my collar are there not for fun. Colonel Star put his life and career on the line for your love.

I want your opinion, would you marry Colonel Star if he was allowed and remain in the Army?" "I would if he was the lowest person to your president. I will follow him through all hardships." Sakusha tells Bast."

"That is good to hear. Miss Chitosa, the world is changing; another war is brewing on the horizon. Your husband will be away for extended times. Do you still want to be with him?" Bast asked. "My reply has not changed. I will wait as long as it takes for his return." Sakusha says. "Well, Mrs. Star, welcome to the family.

I think it is time to let your future husband in on the news, Miss Chitosa-san." General Bast says.

"Colonel Star, you can come in; your wife and I have come to an understanding.

Let me start with refusing to accept your resignation and congratulate you, General Frank Star, on your choice of wife."

"Sir, did you say General?" says Star. "I did, and you do not have to worry about mingling with this Japanese women.

Events in Korea have changed that policy. I have spoken to your lovely future wife about what the future might hold for you. She agrees you should remain in the military.

As a one-star general, you have certain privileges. For example, you have access to all kinds of items for your wedding. So don't forget to invite me." General Bast says.

Sakusha bows to Bast. "It will be an honor to have your presence at our wedding," says Sakusha.

"General Star, here is your star for your collar and orders. Your camp will double in size; I expect your men to be trained and ready for action in three months. If I were you, I would not hesitate with your wedding." suggested General Bast.
Yes, Sir!" General Star salutes.

"Frank, will it get very busy at your camp?" Sakusha asked. "It will, for the both of us. You with your sister and Okina will have to plan the wedding. Anything you need, I'll have someone get it. I have to get the camp ready for thousands more men. Do you have any objections to living with me before we are married?" Star asked Sakusha. She smiles, nodding she does not.

Before leaving, Star mounts a flag with a star on the fender of the staff car.

"Why did you do that?" Sakusha asked. "I think it's time put away with modesty. You will be the General's wife; I want everyone at the base to know.

If your sister still needs work, I can use someone to clean after Okina moves into her new home." Star says. "You do not need a servant; it will be my duty to clean the house," Sakusha tells Star. "Are you sure? I would talk to Okina before you decide." Star suggested.

Arriving at the front gate, the flag with a star gets the guard's immediate attention. Snapping to attention, he salutes. "General Star! "calls out the sentry. "Yes, private, continue your duties." General Star commanded.

Stopping at his quarters, the General notices that Gahou is still on the base.

"Sakusha, let's some have fun?" Frank says. Stepping from the staff car, Star calls out. "Sergeant Major Kazinski, I know you're around! get over here!"

The sergeant rushes from the General's quarters. "Sir!" This time he notices Star's rank. "General! When, Sir?" Never mind when Sergeant Major. I expect you to have the proper rank on your sleeve the next time I see you!" General Star tells him.

"Me, Sergeant Major, Sir?" says Kazinski. "Yes. I go up, so do you.

Now explain to me why Gahou is still on the base? If this continues, I expect you to marry her."

Gahou gives the general a stern gaze. "I do not think so. We are not even close to discussing marriage." Gahou tells Frank.

"I don't expect you to get married at the moment; maybe after Sakusha, are married," Star says. "I thought you were resigning from the military," Gahou says. "It started that way, it turned out more than I expected.

Okina and Hondo stroll over from their quarters. "What is happening?" asked Okina.

"Now that everyone is here, I have important news that affects everyone.

Sakusha and I will be married in a month. Okina, Gahou, I am leaving the details for the event to you and Sakusha. A lot will happen in the future. I will assign someone from the base to assist you with anything you need.

Sergeant Major, this base will double in size and personnel in three months. I want all officers and non-com's in the mess tent for a briefing in one hour.

The world is in for more hurt. You know what I'm talking about, Sergeant Major." General Star tells him. "I do, Sir."

chapter twenty-seven

The long haul

"Attention!" Sergeant Major shouts as he and General Star enters the mess tent.

"At ease. Be seated. I have called you here to inform you we are preparing for another war. This time it's in Korea.

Supplies and troops will arrive soon. I want training and drill programs on my desk by tomorrow.

If you're wondring, this Star on my shoulder comes with a wife if you have not heard. I am getting married to Miss Chitosa, and you are all invited since the wedding will be held here or wherever my wife decides. Dismiss." General Star tells his subordinates.

Leaving the mess tent, Sergeant Major Kazinski is acting a little nervous, which the General pickups on.

"Sergeant Major, is there a problem? You're acting jittery; I hope you're not getting cold feet about fighting." General Star says.

"It's not that, Sir. The order marrying Gahou has me nervous." "Sergeant Major, sometimes committing to someone is more terrifying than rushing a machinegun nest. Don't worry about marrying Gahou, it was a joke. I think she'll be the one proposing when she's ready."

Sakusha is about to get first-hand experience of the General's cleaning habits.

"Okina, I suggested Frank would not need someone to do his cleaning when you move to your home. That duty would fall on me." Sakusha tells her.

"Let me enlighten you what you are in store if you think it will be easy. Follow me to reality." Okina says.

Stepping into the General's bedroom gives Sakusha the shock of her life." Oh my God!" she says. "From your expression, you can see my point," Okina says.

"Is it like this every day?" Sakusha asked. "If I do not keep up with his mess, it is," states Okina. "I will need help. If I hire Kaori, will you train her?" Sakusha asked. "If she'll accept the challenge," says Okina.

1953 General Star returns to Kyoto, waiting for him at the air base is Sakusha and their two children.

With his children in his arms. Frank says, "Two wars are enough. We should live a comfortable life on my retirement in Japan." Sakusha looks at him, agreeing it's time to retire.

"Can we visit America before you retire? I want the children to visit your home before we settle down." "We will, after the wedding. My Sergeant Major is tired of waiting for Gahou to decide what she wants to do." Frank tells his wife.

"Will your Sergeant take Gahou back to America if he marries her?" Sakusha asked. "I don't know. He does have family in America; that's for him and Gahou to discuss."

"Let's go home; I have to make up for lost time with you and the children."

The end

Published through amazons kdp

Cover illustration SelfPubBookCovers.com/ farmhaus

There are many more short stories from this aurthor on amazon.

www.ingramcontent.com/pod-product-compliance
Lightning Source LLC
Chambersburg PA
CBHW061248120726
48001CB00001B/199